SURPRISED BY HER

CHELSEA M. CAMERON

About Surprised By Her

When my boss at Bluebird Pottery, Sydney, left me in charge while she went on vacation with her girlfriend, I wasn't looking forward to it. During my first few hours, a tall, stunning stranger walked in, and I could barely breathe. Of course I ruined everything by spilling coffee all over her. What I didn't expect was for her to push me up against the sink and kiss the hell out of me when I tried to help her clean up in the bathroom.

I never thought I'd see her again, and then she showed up to my book club and introduced herself as Ryan Jewel, the heiress to a candle company fortune and is so far out of my league, we're not even on the same planet. Still, I keep running into her in Arrowbridge, and it doesn't feel like a coincidence.

At first, I'm happy to be sucked into Ryan's glittering orbit. Everything is first class all the way, and it's nice to have a little luxury in my life. Even beyond the money, I'm dazzled by her. Underneath her chilly exterior is someone who's secretly kind, and funny, and who cares fiercely for those she loves.

It doesn't take long for me to completely fall for her, but could this incredible creature ever want a small-town life with someone like me?

Chapter One

"Good morning," I said in my cheerful, customer service voice. I'd perfected it over the past few years working retail, and it was going to be in full force this week. Sydney, my boss and manager, was currently lounging on a beach with her gorgeous girlfriend, and I was just hoping nothing went wrong. Since it was only Monday, I had a lot of hours to go.

A few people came into the shop and I made my presence known, but not too aggressively. They seemed like they were just killing time, so I let them do their thing and did my best not to hover.

The door opened again and in walked a woman who was so tall, I couldn't help but stare. She definitely wasn't from around here. I had only lived in Arrowbridge for five months, but I'd never seen anyone who looked like her. Her hair was so blonde it was almost white, cut short on the sides and longer on top, and carefully styled so she was both glam and butch at the same time.

Icy blue eyes scanned the shop and then stopped when they found me.

"Good morning," I said, my voice barely audible. I cleared my throat and tried again. "Good morning, can I help you?"

She stepped closer and I took in her dark blue short-sleeve button-down, black slacks, and boat shoes.

Tall. So freaking tall. I was only just above five feet, so to me, most people were tall, but she was taller.

She finally spoke. "I'm looking for a gift." Her voice was rich too. Expensive and cultured. Definitely not from here.

"We have all kinds of gift items, maybe I can help you choose something?" I asked. This was one of the best parts of my job. Second only to packing the perfect box for some reason.

She flicked her eyes over my lavender hair, which sometimes people couldn't hide their disapproval about. With her, I only caught a little surprise before she went back to walking around the shop.

"I think I can handle it on my own," she said.

I sighed inwardly. Damn. She was probably going to leave without buying anything. One of my goals this week was to sell as many things as I possibly could to show Sydney and her mom, Eileen (who was also technically my boss) that I was good at my job. They'd given me a chance and I wanted to show them it had been worth it.

"Can I get you a cup of coffee?" I asked. Some days Arrowbridge locals would come in just to grab a free cup, but actual customers loved it too, even though it was June and most people wanted iced drinks.

"Sure," she said, picking up a mug and studying the design on it before setting it back down. There were silver rings on nearly every one of her fingers. The other people who'd been wandering around left, so it was just her and me in the main part of the shop, with Eileen out back painting mugs and listening to music on her headphones.

I filled a cup with black coffee and grabbed some creamer

packets and a stirring stick, as well as a cup sleeve and a napkin.

"Here you are," I said, going to hand her the cup, but I bumped her hand as she reached and the cup ended up spilling all over her front.

She jumped back, but some of the coffee had doused her shirt and pants.

"Oh my god, oh my god," I said, dropping everything. "I'm so sorry, fuck, are you okay?"

"Where's the bathroom?" she asked, and I pointed.

Her legs were so long that she made it to the bathroom quicker than I did and I stood there as she turned on the sink and started dousing herself with water.

Immediately, my thoughts went to panic. What if I'd burned her? Was she going to sue the store? There was no way that Sydney had enough money to pay for a lawsuit and then the business was going to go under and I'd be out of a job.

She cursed a few times under her breath and then unbuttoned her shirt and pulled it off, revealing a white tank top with a beige bra underneath.

"Are you okay?" I asked again as she pulled up the shirt to reveal an absolutely ripped stomach. I'd never seen abs like that up close before. Her skin was red in spots from where it had been splashed by the coffee.

"Fuck," I said, staring to really panic. Why had I given her coffee? Why couldn't I just have left her alone and ogled her from afar? Why did shit like this always seem to happen to me?

"Let me help you," I said, searching for any way I could salvage this situation. I grabbed some towels and wetted them with water and started pressing them against her stomach.

Strong hands took hold of my wrists and stopped me. I looked up, way up, into her face.

"I'm okay," she said. "Nothing a washing machine can't fix."

"But your skin is all red," I said.

"It's fine," she said, pushing my hands away. Oh shit, now I'd fucked up even worse by putting my hand all over her abs.

Beautiful women made me lose my mind, exhibit 1,000.

"I'm so sorry," I said.

"It was an accident," she said, letting go of my hands. "No harm done."

Her mouth kicked up in the briefest of smiles.

"I'm still sorry," I said. "Are you sure you're not burned?"

"The coffee wasn't that hot," she said. "No permanent damage."

"Oh," I said. "Good."

She continued to look down at me as I held the dripping towels in my hands, unable to break my gaze from hers.

I opened my mouth to say something else, but then I couldn't, because she had kissed me.

The towels fell from my grasp as the stranger shoved me against the sink and ravished my mouth.

What. Was. Happening?

IN THE MOMENTS it took me to register that I was being kissed by this very tall and very hot stranger, my instincts took over and I was kissing her back, trying to push myself up to be as tall as I could to get closer to her. That mouth was surprisingly soft and lush and demanding. She attacked me, but it was a coordinated attack. Targeted. As if she knew exactly what she wanted and was going to do whatever it took to get it.

One moment I was struggling to stand and the next she had picked me up and set me on the sink. I yelped a little at the coldness of the marble, but she just swallowed the sound and slid her tongue into my mouth.

This woman was relentless, and I wasn't sure if I would

even survive it. She was so much, too much, but I only craved more. Whatever she wanted to give me, I would take it.

Just as abruptly as the kiss started, it stopped. My eyes fluttered open and I found myself staring deep into those blue eyes.

I opened my mouth to say something, but no words came out.

Slowly she stood back to her full height, gazing down at me. She brushed her thumb across my mouth once.

"Let's just keep that between us," she said, and I found myself nodding. Honestly, I would have agreed to anything she asked of me. Anything.

My entire body was still on fire from the kiss, and my knees wobbled as I tried to hop gracefully down from the sink and stumbled.

She picked up her coffee-soaked shirt and buttoned it with more finesse than I'd ever had in my entire life before opening the door and leaving the bathroom. I followed clumsily after her, trying to find something to say, but failing.

She made it to the door and paused, giving me one last look over her shoulder. The intensity in her eyes pinned me to the spot and took my breath away.

"Have a nice day," I gasped as she pushed through the door and walked down the street.

∽

"HAVE A NICE DAY?" I repeated to myself over and over the rest of the afternoon. What the hell was that? I could have said anything else, *should* have said anything else.

It couldn't have been possible to die from embarrassment, because I would have expired that afternoon from replaying the morning over and over in my mind. I knew I was obsessing, and I needed to break the mental cycle, but I couldn't stop.

Somehow, I made it through the rest of the day without making a further fool of myself and it was a huge relief to lock the door and turn off the lights and say goodbye to Eileen. She'd been in the back making pottery the entire time and had no idea about the coffee spilling or the kiss, and I wasn't going to tell her about it.

I stopped at the grocery store to pick up a few things and headed home, feeling the tension melt off my shoulders. I always felt better when I pulled into my driveway. Safe. I was safe now.

My parents had only owned the house for six months, but that didn't matter. It was home. The farmhouse was built in the 1800s and renovated about five years ago, but it retained so much of the charm of the original house with carved wooden banisters, stone fireplaces, and pretty little windows with stained glass. My favorite part, though, was the porch swing where I spent a lot of time sitting and drinking coffee and reading.

"Hey," I called as I walked through the door and back to the kitchen to set down the groceries.

"How was your day?" a voice said behind me as I opened the fridge. I turned around and found my mom with her arms out for a hug.

"Fine," I lied through my teeth as she hugged me. "Hey, Mama." My other mother came out of her office and approached me for a hug as well.

"You sure it was fine?" Mom asked, tucking some of my hair behind my ears.

"Uh huh," I said, nodding a little too vigorously and then pushing my glasses back up my nose.

They shared a look. One of those parental looks that spoke a thousand words, but in only a language they could understand.

Mama put her arm around Mom and leaned into her.

Visually, they didn't seem to go together. Mom had played softball and had her gray hair cut short and only wore clothes from the LL Bean outlet store. Mama's hair was long and dark brown and she always did something pretty with it. She sold real estate, so she had a closet full of suits and pencil skirts and pretty dresses, but the second she got home it was off with the work clothes and on with the matching sweat set and her old fuzzy socks.

"It was a great day," I said with false enthusiasm.

The two of them just waited. They knew I'd crumble sooner or later. I always did.

"Okay fine, I have never been more embarrassed in my life," I said, leaning down and resting my forehead on the counter.

"What happened?" Mama asked, rubbing my back in soothing motions.

"I was getting coffee for this customer and spilled it all over her," I said, cutting myself off before I could tell them that the customer had kissed the hell out of me after. That part was going with me to the grave.

"Oh sweetie, I'm sure they know it was an accident," Mama said. I stood up and could feel my face blazing.

Normally I told the two of them just about everything, but I couldn't tell them this. My therapist and I had been working on me setting better boundaries with them. I was a grown woman and didn't need to tell my parents every single detail of my life. Easier said than done, though.

"I know, but it was still mortifying," I said.

They both hugged me and then helped me with the rest of the groceries as Mom told me about her day. She was the PE teacher at Hartford High School, and I could always count on her to tell me funny stories about her students.

"So then I said that filming dances to post online doesn't count as exercise and they were really upset about that. I gave them the choice of basketball, badminton, or jump rope," she said as Mama cut up chicken for stir fry.

"I can't believe people are still playing badminton," I said. "It seems so old-fashioned."

Mom shrugged. "It's easy to set up the nets and it doesn't require a ton of expensive equipment or athletic prowess."

"I wasn't good at it," I mumbled.

"You were fine. It's just not your sport," Mom said, slinging her arm around my shoulder.

"What is my sport?" I asked, going through all of the sports I had tried and failed at in my life.

Mom thought about that for a second. "I don't think we've found it yet."

"That's a nice way of saying I suck," I said, slicing through a tomato.

"Hey, don't talk about my daughter that way," Mama said, touching my back.

The three of us settled into our usual dinner routine and then cuddled together on the couch to watch our favorite show.

It wasn't that I didn't want to have a social life or make friends. It was just…really hard.

A year ago, I'd been living in my own apartment a few states away and working remotely doing random jobs, and I'd managed to isolate myself so completely that I barely left the apartment. My lease had been up and my parents had just bought the house and said I could come and have the entire third floor of the house to myself with a gorgeous bathroom and big tub and I could relax and stop worrying about paying rent and just take a pause for a while.

I hadn't been able to say no, even though there wasn't much in the way of a social scene in Arrowbridge. There were a lot of queer people, which was why my parents had looked at it as a potential place to move. The two of them had made tons of friends already and had a much better social life than I could ever hope for.

Sydney, my boss, had invited me to hang with her friends, but I hadn't been able to get up the nerve to do it yet. I'd flaked a few times, but she hadn't seemed offended when I canceled at the last minute, so I had hope that, one day, I could make it happen.

After the show, I went upstairs and slid into my bathtub with a lavender bath bomb.

"You'd better fix my life," I said to it as I dropped it into the water.

No such luck, but it did help me relax a tiny bit.

I couldn't stop thinking about the stranger and what the hell had possessed her to just kiss me like that. Was she the kind of person who walked around kissing people? Had she done it as a joke? Was it part of some viral internet trend I didn't know about?

All kinds of possibilities flitted through my mind as I came up with increasingly more outlandish and truly mean reasons for her to have kissed me.

If there was one sport I excelled at, it was jumping to the worst possible conclusion. Always.

I was going to have a lot to talk about with my therapist this week.

Chapter Two

I WAS jumpy for the next day at work. I couldn't stop waiting and expecting the stranger to come back and explain herself. Every time the door opened, I would flinch and it was exhausting. Somehow, I made it through the day, but it was rough.

On Wednesday, a familiar face walked in with twin girls.

"Hey," I said as Layne looked around and smiled when she saw me. The twins were glued to their phones and barely looked up.

"Hey, how are you doing managing all this by yourself?" Layne was one of the kindest people I'd met. The only other one who was kinder was her friend Joy, who worked a few shops down the street at Mainely Books. I'd already spent way too much of my meager paycheck there on books since I'd moved here.

"I'm surviving," I said, trying to laugh.

"Hey, the place looks great, so that's something," she said, looking around. "We're out and about today and I thought I'd check in."

"Did Sydney ask you to?" I asked, a little suspicious. I

didn't like the idea that Sydney would send her friends in to look in on me to make sure I wasn't fucking this up too badly.

"No, she's too busy, I think," Layne said. "If you know what I mean."

I snorted, thinking about how Sydney and Lark were like. "Oh, I know exactly what you mean."

"Honor is trying not to check up on them too much, but Lark has barely texted her since they got to the island," Layne said, rolling her eyes. "One thing's for sure, everyone knows who the strict mom is going to be between the two of us. Not that we're ready for that, we need to get married first." Layne looked down at her sparkling ring and smiled.

"Anyway, I actually have a reason for being here. Mark's niece, Ryan, is visiting for a few months and I wanted to get her a little welcome gift, so I'm putting together a basket with lots of Arrowbridge things." Layne was too sweet.

"What were you thinking?" I asked her.

"She definitely needs a lobster mug," Layne said, grabbing one and setting it on the counter with the register. "Two mugs." She added another lobster mug to the other one.

Layne fluttered around the shop and I just let her do her thing as she added more items to her collection.

The twins would look up every now and then and comment before going back to their phones.

"They're at that age," Layne said as I rung her up. "I know they're bored, and they want to be with their friends, but I miss when they were younger and they would talk my ears off." She sighed and shook her head. "Pretty soon they'll be dating and getting jobs and driving and I'll be obsolete."

"I'm sorry," I said. That had to be hard, taking care of the kids their whole lives and then just being out of a job.

Layne waved her hands. "It's not your problem to worry about. Oh, I wanted to invite you over on Saturday. We're having a little party partially to welcome Ryan, but also just because."

The idea of a party made my stomach drop to my feet and I could feel the excuses clamoring at the back of my throat. It was pure muscle memory to start giving excuses for why I couldn't come.

Instead of what I always did, I swallowed those words and gave myself a second. The panic continued to ramp up, but I forced myself to speak.

"I'd love to," I gasped out, hiding my shaking hands behind my back. "What time?"

Layne either didn't notice the chaos that was going on with me, or she pretended not to.

"Perfect. It's at two, and you don't need to bring anything, just your purple-haired self," she said, grinning at me. "Girls, say goodbye to Everly," Layne prompted.

"Bye," they said in perfect unison before waving, also exactly the same way.

"I'm starving," one of the twins said as they walked through the door.

"Me too," the other one said.

"Okay, let's get you some lunch," Layne said with a laugh.

"I'M MIGHT GO to a party on Saturday," I announced to my parents when I got home from work that night as we sat on the couch watching our nightly shows.

They shared a look of surprise.

"You are?" Mama said slowly.

"I am," I said, nodding. "Layne, Sydney's friend, invited me over for a little party Saturday at two and I'm going to go. I know I have book club tomorrow night, but I think I can do both."

"Sweetie, that's wonderful," Mom said, giving me a hug.

"Thanks," I said. "Here's hoping I actually make it there."

Agreeing to an event was the first step. Getting my ass there was the bigger challenge.

"You have your meds if you need them and you have your list," Mama reminded me.

"I know," I said. My therapist and I had developed a list of things I could do that helped me get out of an anxiety spiral. That, in addition to my meds and other coping strategies, were my arsenal for fighting my brain when it acted up.

"I'm really proud of you," Mama said, kissing my temple.

"I'm proud of me too," I said. That was something else I'd been working on.

"I think we should celebrate this," Mom said, getting up from the couch. "I'm getting out the champagne."

"Mom, we don't need champagne," I said, but she was already heading to the kitchen with Mama on her heels. They were absolutely going to talk about me, but that was fine.

Negative voices in my head wanted to tell me that agreeing to go to a party wasn't anything to celebrate. That I was a ridiculous loser who couldn't do normal things just like everyone else without having a panic attack.

I closed my eyes and did some quick breathing exercises until Mom and Mama came back with the glasses of bubbly.

"Cheers," Mom said, and we all clinked our glasses together.

"We can make some dip for you to bring with you," Mama said.

"Layne told me that it was taken care of and I shouldn't bring anything. Besides, you're already making it for book club," I said.

"Oh," Mama said, her face falling.

"You can make us dip," Mom said, kissing her cheek. "We'll have our own party."

Mama's eyes lit up. "We haven't done that in a long time."

Anyone could see the spark between them, and I felt my face getting red as they kissed passionately.

"Okay, can you not be all like that in front of me?" I said and they both laughed.

"You know when you get annoyed, that just makes us want to do it more?" Mom said, her eyes gleaming.

I stood up from the couch. "Okay, it's time for me to go to my room and read."

"Goodnight," Mama sang before dissolving into giggles.

"Wait until I leave the room!" I yelled, not turning around.

"YOU READY?" Mama asked me as I grabbed the tray of dips she'd made that I was bringing with me to book club. Tonight I had roasted red pepper, tzatziki, and cowboy caviar, along with bags of chips. Someone else always brought a veggie tray, so that was already covered.

"I am," I said as I grabbed everything. "I'll see you when I get back."

"Have fun," Mom called from the living room.

"I will," I said.

Most social situations set off my anxiety, and book club was no exception, but this was my fourth one, and I knew the ropes by now. The group was low-pressure, so I didn't feel the need to talk, or have the spotlight on me, which helped a lot. Plus, we were talking about books, which was a whole lot easier than having to talk about myself, or my life, or anything super personal.

This month's book was an older young adult book that was a gorgeous sapphic Cinderella retelling that I had already read lots of times but was happy to read again. We read both old and new releases, so it was fun to go back to something that was a bit older and see it with fresh eyes.

Everyone in the group was absolutely lovely, but I'd yet to make any really strong connections with people to hang out after book club. Right now I was just getting used to being a part of the group and contributing what I could. Oh, and bringing the dip.

I managed to make it to book club at a reasonable time, instead of almost an hour early like I had the first two times I'd come. That had been completely embarrassing, but I'd just pretended like I'd wanted to come early to help out if I could.

Joy was the first person I saw and she immediately took the tray with the dip bowls and the bags of chips from me.

"Sometimes in between meetings, I dream about these dips," she said. "Is that weird?"

Joy had medium brown hair that fell straight down her back and the kindest energy. I loved coming to the bookstore whenever I could, and she always found something new and interesting for me to read.

"I can ask for some of the recipes, but I don't think she's going to want to give them up," I said with a laugh.

Joy tapped her chin as if she was thinking.

"What are you doing over here? You look like you're plotting," Ezra said, coming over. When I'd first met her, I'd been a little intimidated. It wasn't every day you met someone with knuckle tattoos. She also seemed like the kind of person who held herself back when she first met you, something I could really understand. Some people might think of Ezra as chilly, but I didn't see her that way, especially when she was with Joy.

"Just trying to figure out how I can get Everly's mom to give me some of her dip recipes," Joy said.

"She always jokes that I'll get them in her will," I said. "She won't even let me in the kitchen when she's making them."

"Hmmm," Joy said, frowning. "I'll think of something. In the meantime..." she trailed off and went to get the chips on the snack table along with the dips.

"Would you like a drink?" Ezra asked me.

"Yeah, that would be great. Non-alcoholic."

She winked. "Coming right up."

I headed to the back of the bookstore, which had an open space where the chairs were set up. Lots of people were here already, talking in small groups and already munching on snacks and sampling the drinks. Joy went above and beyond and usually did themed decorations and drinks and a cake every month. It was a lot of work for a club that was free to join.

I said hello to a few other people and found a seat. Ezra returned with my drink and handed it over.

"Thanks so much," I said, taking it from her.

"You're welcome."

Joy called everyone to order a few minutes later, and my stomach started to churn a little. I told myself that I'd done this before, I knew the process, and I wasn't required to do anything I didn't want to. If all I was up for was sitting in my chair and eating and drinking and not even saying a word about the book, I could do that and no one would say a damn thing.

"Wait just a second," Layne said, looking up from her phone as Joy opened the floor up for initial impressions of the book.

"We have one more who's just parking her car," Layne said and a few seconds later the bell above the door jingled as someone walked in. My back was to the front and I turned around to see who it was.

It was the stranger I kissed.

"Everyone, this is Ryan, Ryan, this is everyone," Layne said as I tried to calm the hell down.

"Oh," I said accidentally as Ryan walked toward the group. She didn't have a book with her, but a lot of people read ebooks so they didn't have a book with them.

This was the Ryan she was having the party for? The tall, hot stranger? The stranger who had kissed me on Monday?

"Sorry I'm late," she said, looking around for a spare seat. There were three options, including one on my right and that was the one she chose. Her legs were so long that she stretched them out in front of her. If I sat all the way back on my chair, my feet didn't touch the ground. Calling Ryan "imposing" was an understatement. How the hell had we both fit in that tiny bathroom?

The thought of being with her in the bathroom at the pottery shop made my face go red.

Ryan hadn't acknowledged me, just kept her focus on Joy as she started over and people spoke about how they'd liked the book, and what their biggest takeaways had been.

With Ryan next to me, I absolutely couldn't focus on what anyone was saying. She sucked away all of my attention. Tonight she wore athletic pants that did nothing to hide her rock-hard thighs. I'd seen a video once of a woman crushing a watermelon between her thighs and that was all I could think of as Joy asked discussion questions and people responded. There was no way I could form any coherent thought with Ryan beside me. Not a chance.

Then she spoke, talking about some obscure book she'd read that reminded her of a scene in this book and I had a good reason to look at her and that just made everything worse.

Everything about her was interesting, from her fiery blue eyes to the way she gestured as she talked, to the words she said. Ryan may not have gone to Yale, but I would bet all the money in my bank account she went to another fancy college, or at the very least was accomplished enough to get into one.

I'd just gone to a small state school to get my degree in communications that I hadn't really ended up using when I'd ventured into the crowded job market. Retail and sales jobs were all I could find, so I dove in, and had bounced around ever since. Now I was full-time at Bluebird Pottery and while I didn't see it as a forever job, it was perfect for now. Sydney gave me a lot of freedom, and I loved packing boxes out back and chatting with Eileen as she worked. She had all kinds of interesting stories, and we got along really well. From what Sydney had alluded to, her mom didn't get along with a lot of people. Eileen got lost in her own head a lot, and sometimes you'd be in the middle of a conversation and she'd just float away, completely forgetting about you. As someone neurodivergent, I sympathized, and I didn't take any of it personally. Brains were strange and unique, and Eileen did things in her own way, in her own time.

Ryan finished speaking and I had to remind myself to breathe. She readjusted her legs and I had to look away so everyone didn't read the lewd thoughts on my face that I was having about those legs.

For the first time, I was almost relieved when the discussion part of book club was over and it was time to eat and talk and drink before going home.

Since I had the option of having the dips anytime I wanted, I left them for other people and hit the desserts, including the cake, which had a picture of the book cover on it and beautiful swirls of frosting around the edges. It was from Sweet's Sweets Bakery, located in the neighboring town of Castleton, and I'd never had cake that good in my life. Each one was not only a work of art, but a spiritual experience to eat.

I loaded up my plate with the intention of having some now, but taking most of it home, including an extra piece of cake for Mom and Mama to share, as they requested.

I was just grabbing another macaron when I felt someone standing behind me and saw a shadow fall across the table. Such a massive shadow could only belong to one person. I took a breath for strength before I turned around to face her.

"Hi," I said. "Um, it's nice to meet you. Again."

"Nice to meet you..." she trailed off, waiting for me to say my name.

"Everly," I said, looking up at her. "I'm Everly."

"Everly," she said, her voice wrapping around my name like a warm blanket on a cold night. "It's nice to officially meet you."

She put her hand out, her wrist gleaming with an expensive watch.

"It's nice to meet you too," I managed to say as she shook my hand. Her fingers were incredibly warm and soft and for the few seconds she touched me, everything in my head just went completely quiet.

She reached around me to grab a plate and I smelled a clean, almost woodsy green scent that made me think of moss. It was delicious.

"How's the cake at these things?" she asked.

"It's heaven," I said.

"In that case," she said, cutting a large piece and setting it on her plate.

"Fan of cake?" I asked.

"You could say that," she said, grabbing a fork.

"What kind of cake is your favorite?" I asked.

She thought about that for a moment. "My grandmother used to make something called hummingbird cake that I loved. It has pineapple and bananas and pecans with cream cheese frosting," she said.

"Ohhh, that sounds good. I've never heard of it," I said.

"It's a southern thing," she said. "My grandmother was born in South Carolina, so I think she got it from her family."

"I'd love to try it," I said, and she took a bite of the cake. This one was just a classic marble cake with vanilla and chocolate with a whipped cream frosting. Simple and delicious.

Ryan closed her eyes and I swear she let out the tiniest little noise that hit me so hard that I almost fell over.

"That is good," she said after she'd swallowed.

"It is," I said.

"So," she said after another bite, "how long have you been in the book club?"

"Not that long. I needed a little convincing to join," I admitted. Oops.

"Why?"

I opened my mouth to lie, slammed it shut, and then tried again. "Social situations are hard for me."

I couldn't meet her eyes and waited for her to find a way to extricate herself from the conversation. A lot of people bailed after hearing about that.

"That must be really difficult," she finally said, and I could tell she'd chosen her words with care. Our eyes met and I studied her.

"It is," I said. "If I don't force myself, I'll just stay in the house and not talk to anyone or see anyone and get completely separated from the rest of the world."

I didn't normally tell people I'd just met this much information about me, but there was something about Ryan. Sure, she was physically imposing, but it was easy to talk to her for some reason.

"It can be easy to shut out the world," she said. "Or to surround yourself with only a few people."

She got it. I could tell she got it.

"Why did you decide to come to book club?" I asked.

"Layne forced me," she said, and for the first time I saw her smile softly.

Help. I was having an emergency. Ryan's smile was better

than cake. It was gone quickly, but I burned it in the back of my mind so I could keep it.

"I'm not surprised. Sydney didn't really give me an option not to join either. She was nice about it, but she really pestered me to come until I did. I'm glad she did, though."

I didn't regret coming to book club at all. It was setting the foundation for me to be more part of the world again. A baby step on the way to bigger steps. My job had been the first huge hurdle. The party on Saturday was yet another step.

"So am I," she said, and there was that heat again. Was this flirting?

"Sorry to interrupt," Joy said, coming over. "We're getting ready to clean up. You don't have to leave, just wanted to let you know."

"Oh, yeah, of course," I said, feeling my face go red and my anxiety starting to escalate. I didn't want to make Joy's life difficult.

Ryan pulled me aside by one of the shelves.

"We should talk," she said.

"Right," I said.

"Not here," she said, her eyes flicking around. "I'd rather have some privacy."

"Yeah, definitely," I said, nodding.

"Are you coming to Layne's party this weekend?"

"I might," I said, even though I had already agreed.

Ryan leaned against a shelf and gazed down at me. "You should."

Over the years of me canceling plans with people, gradually they would just stop asking. It had been a long time since someone had asked me to come to something like this. Layne inviting me felt more like her just being nice or feeling pity for me. Ryan inviting me was completely different.

"How tall are you?" I blurted out.

"Six-three," she said, which made her more than an entire

foot taller than me. Standing in front of her made it feel like more.

"Congratulations," I said for some reason.

She let out a soft sound that was almost a laugh. "Thank you, although I can't say I'm responsible. I come from tall ancestors."

"Lucky," I said.

"Not always."

All I wanted was to keep talking to her in this bookstore, but I also needed to get the cake home to my parents and they did need to close up.

Ryan let out a long breath. "I should go."

"Me too," I said.

She seemed like she was going to say something else, but then shook her head.

"It was nice to see you again, Everly," she said.

"Without spilling anything this time," I said.

"Maybe next time I can get you back," she said.

She could spill anything and everything on me that she wanted, but I managed not to say that out loud.

When I didn't respond, she said, "See you later, Everly."

"Bye," I gasped out, as she walked over to the group cleaning up and said goodbye. She gave me one last look when she opened the door and left.

My body sagged against the bookshelf.

Chapter Three

I WOKE on Saturday morning with my stomach already churning. I reached over for one of my anxiety pills and the bottle of water I kept on my nightstand. Today I was going to need it. I'd had an edible last night to help me sleep so I hadn't been awake all night.

As I lay in bed, I tried to think of nice things to calm my racing heart until the meds kicked in. Once that happened, I could hopefully eat something for breakfast so I didn't head to the party with a rumbling stomach.

I went downstairs and found my parents in the kitchen, making breakfast and singing along with old country songs.

"Good morning, how are you feeling?" Mama said, coming over to give me a hug. She wore a frilly apron that was covered in flour.

"So far, so good," I said.

"You sure?" Mama said, holding my face in her hands and looking into my eyes.

"Yes," I said. "I'm good."

"That's what I want to hear," she said, kissing my forehead. In the past I had lied about how debilitating my anxiety was when I talked to my parents. It was only after they'd observed me having a panic attack in a restaurant that they'd realized it was as bad as it was.

"Do you want some pancakes, sweetie?" Mom asked as she flipped several chocolate chip pancakes in the pan. The timer went off and Mama pulled a tray of bacon out of the oven.

"Um, not yet," I said. "But how about some tea?"

"Coming right up," Mama said, filling the electric kettle to heat the water up. Normally I drank coffee, but it had a tendency to make my anxiety worse, so I was going to skip it for today.

I sat at the dining table as Mama brought me some tea and I practiced my breathing. Being with my parents helped to distract my mind from spiraling, so I focused on the two of them as they talked to me and sang and danced as they cooked.

"We'll keep a plate warm for you," Mom said, making up a plate for me and sticking it in the warm oven.

They ate with me and talked about this and that and all kinds of silly things to keep me distracted.

An hour later, I was able to choke down some pancakes and bacon and gulp a glass of water. I took a long shower and washed my hair before drying and styling it and putting on the outfit that I'd picked out last night. The dress was cute and flowy, with a pattern of geometric bumble bees on it and my brown sandals that were worn in to perfectly shape my feet.

I had my bathing suit in case I got really wild and wanted to jump in the pool and put my hair up in a high pony with a few pieces curling in front. All I needed were my prescription sunglasses and I was set for the afternoon.

My hands shook a little as I tried to put my earrings in my ears and I had to brace my hands on the dresser and take a break.

I was determined not to back down from this challenge.

Things like this party would only get easier the more I did them. It was like lifting weights.

"You've got this," I told myself in the mirror over my dresser. "You've got this."

I grabbed my bag and headed down the stairs.

"I'm heading out," I called.

"Have a good time! Call us if you need anything," Mama called from the kitchen. She and Mom were defrosting the freezer and weeding through the pantry. I wasn't going to miss having to help.

"Love you," I said, blowing them a kiss before heading out to my car.

Hot and cold waves passed through my body as I turned my car on and pulled onto the road.

Mark's house was in a more secluded area, but it was still only a few minutes from my parent's house. I put on my turn signal for the road and then just…kept driving. The ride hadn't been long enough. I needed more prep time, so I drove a little bit longer and then turned around and went back.

This time, I joined the other cars that were already parked. I was still pretty early, which often happened when I was anxious.

I deep breathed for a few seconds before getting out and heading toward the music and sounds of voices in the back of the large home. I'd seen pictures of the place on Layne's social media account, but the reality of the house was far more grand.

There was an assortment of adults all hanging in and around the pool, but I recognized Layne and Honor right away, along with Joy and her girlfriend, Ezra.

My entire body was vibrating as I carefully walked toward them, hoping I didn't trip, and wishing that no one would even look in my direction.

"Hey, I'm so glad you made it," Layne said, giving me a bright smile. "Did you want a drink or something?"

"Water?" I choked out.

"Sure, do you want ice?"

I nodded.

"Be right back," she said, squeezing my arm.

"I am obsessed with this dress," Joy said, sipping a bright pink drink through her straw.

"Thanks," I said, swirling the skirt. "Part of the proceeds go to help save the bees."

There, that was a perfectly normal thing to say. I was killing this so far.

"You're going to have to send me a link. I definitely need that," Joy said. "Don't you think I need that?"

"Definitely," Ezra said with a laugh.

"They sell skirts too," I added as Layne came back with my water.

"I decided to make it festive," she said, pointing to the umbrella and the neon yellow straw.

"Thank you," I said, slowly sipping on the water so I didn't choke and looking around to see if I could find a corner to hide in.

"I wish Syd was here, but I'm glad she's taking a vacation," Layne said.

"Me too, but I'm definitely ready for her to be back," I said. She would be back to her regular job as my boss on Tuesday and I couldn't wait.

"I bet you are," Joy said, laughing.

"Oh my god, finally," Layne said, looking over to the other side of the pool. I turned around and almost dropped my glass of water.

There was Ryan.

She came over wearing a light blue polo shirt and white shorts as if she'd just stepped off a golf course. Her aviator sunglasses were so effortlessly cool that I had to lock my knees so I didn't just melt into a puddle right there.

Ryan pulled off her sunglasses slowly and then hooked them on her shirt. Her blue eyes were completely unreadable, but they were fixed on me. Shit, she was tall.

We were interrupted by a squealing sound as the twins hauled themselves out of the pool and launched themselves toward Ryan, who put out her hand and said, "red light."

The two girls skidded to a stop, crashing into each other.

Ryan reached toward two chairs where some towels were stacked and pulled out two, handing them over to the twins. They dutifully wrapped themselves up.

"Thank you, Auntie Ryan," one of the twins said. I couldn't keep them straight in my head, but I was going to figure it out one of these days.

"You're welcome," she said, giving them a fond look. She sighed. "I can't believe how grown you both are."

The girls preened and started babbling at the same time.

"They just love her," Layne said. "They're so excited she's going to be here for the summer so they can pester her."

Ryan shot Layne a look and then flicked her eyes over to me. I felt my cheeks go red.

"And that's my signal that she needs a drink," Layne said.

"I've got it, babe," Honor said, touching Layne's shoulder.

"Negroni," Layne told her.

"I remember," Honor said, smiling before turning around and heading inside.

Layne watched Honor walk away with a somewhat dazed look on her face.

"She's so hot, I can't believe I get to marry her," she said, shaking her head.

"I know what you mean," Joy said, gazing at Ezra.

"We're not getting married," Ezra said, and then added "yet."

That set off a flurry of excitement from Joy, but I was busy watching Ryan with the twins. She'd sat down on one of the chairs to bring herself closer to their level.

I wanted to talk to her. I wanted to stand near her. I wanted to watch her face and see her smile and I desperately wanted to kiss her again. The last one had been such a blur, I needed another chance. Kisses like that just didn't come along every day. I had to see if it was a fluke or if it was something else.

Too bad she was probably never going to get her lips near my lips again. Since she was Mark's niece, she was fancy and probably rich. I'd known she had money from that first day, but now her wealth was put in perspective and it was much more than I initially thought.

People like Ryan didn't kiss people like me unless it was on a whim or to see what it was like to lock lips with a commoner once and then go back to their regular diamond-studded champagne lives.

Honor returned with Ryan's drink and she took it and gave Honor her thanks.

The twins ran off to talk to someone else, releasing Ryan. She came back over to our group.

"What is even in a negroni?" I blurted out.

Ryan held her glass out to me. "Take a sip and find out."

"Oh, no, I couldn't," I said.

"I can get you one if you want to try it," Layne said.

"I'm better at making them than you are," Honor said.

"You really don't have to do that," I said, but Honor was already walking away.

Shit. I didn't want to be a nuisance. I didn't want people to think I was being demanding or rude.

In spite of my meds, my chest was starting to feel tight and I had that tingle in my hands that told me that I was starting to lose it.

"Where's the bathroom?" I managed to ask Layne.

"I'll show you," she said, studying my face and then taking my arm.

I let Layne lead me into the house and down the hall to a bathroom.

"You okay?" she asked. I gave her a jerky nod and closed the door.

I paced the room before putting down the lid of the toilet and sitting down, putting my head between my knees. My heart beat so fast that it felt like it was trying to escape from my chest.

I hated this fucking feeling so much. Things had been going so well and I'd relaxed too much and here I was, in the bathroom, my stomach roiling like a storm and my body sending up all the danger signals.

Breathe. I needed to breathe. Logically I knew that a panic attack could only last a maximum of twenty minutes, but I had no plans for staying in this bathroom to wait it out. I was going to get my shit together and go back out to this party.

I closed my eyes and did my breathing exercises, counting as I inhaled, held my breath, and then exhaled slowly. That was all I needed to do right now. Breathe.

Time passed. I had no idea how much, but at least no one was pounding on the door and demanding to use the facilities. That had happened more times than I could count and could send me right back into the thick of it.

Somehow, after what I hoped was only a few minutes, my nervous system started to come down from peak panic. I opened my eyes and flexed my fingers. My hand went to my heart and it started to beat a little more normally.

Before I left and threw myself back into the fray, I wanted to give myself a little more time to make sure I wasn't just going to tip over the edge again.

I stood up and realized I'd set my water on the sink counter, so I grabbed it and had a few sips. I also checked myself in the mirror. My face was washed out, so I pinched my cheeks to bring some color back into them.

Figuring it was a good idea, I washed my hands with warm water and then braced myself before I turned the doorknob and left the room.

The hallway was blocked by someone very tall.

"Oh," I said, surprised to see anyone. "I'm sorry, were you waiting for the bathroom?"

Ryan was leaning casually against the wall.

"No," she said.

"Okay," I said. Then why had she been standing here. "Were you waiting for me?"

She opened her mouth, closed it, and then tried again.

"I thought we should talk," she said. "But we don't have to right now."

"No, it's fine," I said.

"There's a guest room right there," she said, pointing down the hall.

I nodded and turned, walking toward it with Ryan following me.

The room was decorated beautifully and looked like no one was staying in it.

Ryan closed the door, and I sat down on the bed. Ryan filled up the room, and I couldn't help but stare.

I set my water on the nightstand, making sure to set it on a coaster so it didn't leave a ring.

Ryan looked around and finally ended up sitting next to me at the end of the bed. It dipped so much that I had to stop myself from sliding right into her. She leaned forward with her elbows on her knees and looked straight ahead.

After a few seconds of silence, I said, "So…"

"So," Ryan said. "Everly."

"That's me," I said, and then wanted to cringe.

Ryan turned her head to look at me.

"I didn't expect to see you again," she said.

"Me neither," I said. "I thought you were probably just passing through. You didn't seem like someone who would be in Arrowbridge for a long time."

She tilted her head to the side slightly. "What does that mean?"

"You're obviously from away," I said, using my hand to indicate her outfit and attitude in general.

"From away? Is that what you call it?" she asked.

"Well, I'm technically from away, but I'm able to fake it," I said.

"But I can't," she said, more a statement than a question.

"Sorry?" I said.

"I feel like I should be insulted," she said.

"It's not your fault," I said. "Mainers are just weird that way."

"Where are you from?" she asked, and I had the sensation that every single ounce of her focus was completely on me. It was like being examined and I hoped that I passed.

"I'm just a Masshole transplant," I said. "I haven't even lived here for a year."

"You don't have much of an accent," she said.

"It comes out in certain situations," I said. "Maybe I'll bust it out for you later."

Was I flirting? Was *this* flirting?

Ryan studied me for a moment in that way she had.

"Where are you from?" I asked.

"Connecticut," she said.

I nodded. "That makes sense."

She let out a little snort that was almost a laugh. "Why is that?"

"Oh, you just give off that Connecticut vibe. Yale, yachts, all that."

"I didn't go to Yale," she said.

"But you've played polo at least once, haven't you?" I asked.

Her jaw clenched just a little. "Yes."

"Sorry, we got a little off track. I think you wanted to talk about things other than where we're from," I said.

"I just wanted to apologize to you for what happened at the store. I have no idea what came over me, I'm not normally like that at all," she said.

"Me neither," I said. "I don't normally make out with strangers that I've just spilled coffee on. You didn't have any burns, did you?"

She shook her head. "No. My skin was a little red, but no permanent damage done."

"Good," I said, letting out a breath. "I'm really sorry about that."

"It's fine. I'm sorry about the kiss," she said.

It was on the edge of my tongue to say *I'm not*, but I managed to keep my mouth shut.

"It's okay. You made the day more exciting, that's for sure," I said with a laugh.

"That's something," she said, looking down at her hands. Her fingers were long and sprinkled with just a few freckles. There was a simple black metallic ring on her right ring finger. Nothing on her left. Not that I was looking.

"How long are you staying in Arrowbridge?" I asked.

"For the summer. I needed a change," she said.

"A change from…" I said, trailing off.

She turned to look at me again. "Everything."

I nodded. "I know exactly what you mean. I moved here for a new start." I didn't tell everyone that I still lived with my parents, because sometimes they got a little weird about it. They'd also ask further questions about why I wasn't out on my own and I didn't like to get into my anxiety stuff right off the bat.

"How is it going?" she asked, finally turning to really face me.

I laughed. "It's going. Sorry, I should have lied."

"No, I prefer honesty to fake sentiment," she said.

"I agree," I said.

This time, my heart beat faster not because of a panic attack. Being with Ryan affected my body, but in the opposite way as my anxiety. Warmth washed through me and my skin tingled as if in anticipation and I couldn't help but lean closer to her, inhaling her scent.

I couldn't put my finger on what exactly Ryan smelled like, but I could sum it up in one word: expensive.

Ryan swallowed and then closed her eyes for a second. "We should get back."

"Of course," I said. I had no idea how long we'd been gone. She stood up and so did I.

"You're really tall," I blurted out.

"I am," she said. "And you're sized just right."

Something about the way she said it coupled with the way she looked down at me made my blood warm and race.

"Am I?" I asked, my voice barely a whisper.

She let out a breath that was almost a sigh. "You are."

The moment shattered at the sound of a phone going off. Ryan pulled a phone out of her pocket, her eyes reading the message.

"We should get back to the party," she said, stepping around me and opening the door.

Mechanically I followed her down the hall and back out to the noise of the pool outside.

I MANAGED to stay another hour at the party before I hit my limit and had to make my excuses and leave. Exhaustion settled on me like a weighted blanket the second I got in my car. By the time I got home, all I wanted to do was lay down and not speak for a while.

I walked through the door and didn't see my parents, so I figured they were in the backyard tending the garden, so I went to check and then sent them both a text that I was back, and I needed some space.

Since I hadn't eaten much at the party, I made myself a little snack plate and took it to the living room and put on an old movie and covered myself in a blanket, even though it was the middle of summer. It was times like these when I wished I had a pet. A dog or cat that would curl up on me.

I wondered if Ryan was still at the party. After we'd talked in the guest room, she'd hung out with our group, but she'd barely said anything. Questions about her had burned in the back of my mind, but I hadn't wanted to be a pest, so I'd kept them all to myself.

Asking Layne was a possibility, but she might read too much into my interest in Ryan. Did Layne know about the kiss? I didn't think so. Ryan seemed like she wanted to keep that between us and completely forget about it.

Only one problem: I was never forgetting about that kiss.

SOMEONE KNOCKED on the wall a while later. "Dinner's ready, sweetie," Mama said in a soft voice.

"Okay," I said, levering myself off the couch. I'd gotten a second wind and was feeling back to my old self.

"How was the party?" she asked as we both headed for the kitchen to grab plates.

"It was good," I said. "I had a moment, but it passed. I socialized and everything."

Mama pulled me into a hug. "Good for you."

"Thanks," I said, hugging her back.

Mom handed me a plate and I filled my plate before heading to the dining room.

"Did you meet anyone new?" Mom asked as she and Mama sat down.

"Um, a few people," I said. There was no way that I could leave out seeing Ryan again, but I had to bring her up carefully.

"That customer I spilled the coffee on was there. The party was actually sort of for her," I said, carefully stabbing a spinach leaf and crouton with my fork.

"She was? What a small world," Mom said.

"Yeah. I said I was sorry about the coffee and she told me she didn't have any burns or anything, so it's all good," I said, cautiously looking up from my plate.

"Maybe you two could be friends," Mama said.

"Maybe," I said. Being friends with Ryan didn't seem like something that was going to happen. She and I were from completely different worlds. Sure, we might interact at book club, but I talked to a lot of people there that I wouldn't be friends with or have contact with otherwise.

"You never know," Mom said.

Chapter Four

"I'm so glad you're back," I told Sydney when I walked through the door of Bluebird Pottery on Tuesday.

"Hello to you too," she said with a laugh, tossing her dark curls over her shoulder. "The shop looks beautiful, and Mom is still alive and well-fed."

"I made her eat lunch every day," I said.

"You are an angel sent from above," Sydney said with a laugh.

"I wouldn't go that far, but thank you anyway," I said. "Enough about me, how was your trip?"

I'd barely heard anything from her the whole week, and I'd just assumed she'd been too busy at the resort and with her love.

"You look like you got some sun." Her skin was just a few shades darker.

"I did. Got burned the first day and got lectured by Lark about the dangers of skin cancer. I told her it was her fault for distracting me so much with her beauty that I'd forgotten to use sunscreen."

"How did she take that?" I asked as I followed her around

the shop, checking everything and making sure we were ready to open for the day. Eileen was already in the back, glazing away to churn out more pottery for the shop and our online orders and to replace the pieces we sold at a few places on consignment.

Sydney grinned. "She was both mad and flattered, so it worked out."

She told me more about the resort and the food and drinks and showed me pictures and video she'd taken. Sydney and Lark were smiling and so in love that it jumped out at you.

"Is Lark back to work today?" I asked.

"Yeah," Sydney said, flipping the Closed sign to Open. "She loved ordering coffee she didn't have to make for a change, but now it's back to the grind."

A few people walked in and we didn't really get to chat again for a while. Summer in Arrowbridge might not be as busy as in other towns closer to the coast, but we did get a rush, and the energy in the shop was noticeably different than it had been when I'd started earlier this year.

I watched the shop while Sydney went upstairs for her lunch break, and then it was my turn. I usually brought leftovers and would eat with Eileen, or head outside if the weather was nice. Sometimes I would cram a sandwich in a few minutes and take a walk outside up and down the street. On days when I had therapy via a video chat, I'd go upstairs and use Sydney's apartment for privacy.

The afternoon lull was my next chance to talk with Sydney.

"No drama while I was gone?" she asked.

"Nope," I said, not meeting her eyes. Since things were good with Ryan, I thought it was best not to mention the coffee spilling incident. It would cause her to ask more questions that I didn't want to answer. She obviously hadn't said anything to Layne or anyone else, so it seemed best to let it go.

"Damn, that's no fun," she said.

"I'm just glad I didn't screw anything up," I said. I'd checked the receipts and balanced everything multiple times to make sure I hadn't messed up the money.

"No, you're annoyingly competent," Sydney said. "I'm so glad that you walked in here and asked for a job. I don't know what I would do without you." Sydney said things like that to me all the time and I was still working on trying to get myself to believe she was sincere.

"Oh, how was that party this weekend? I heard you went," she said.

"I did. It was fun. Lowkey, which was good for me."

"You did book club and a party in the same week? Go you," she said. Over the time I'd worked for her, Sydney had gotten me to open up about my anxiety and my struggles. It hadn't been easy, but she'd been completely amazing about everything, and now I felt comfortable sharing a little bit more about my goals to socialize.

"Yeah, it was a lot last week," I said. "But I lived."

"You absolutely did. I hope you had some cake or something to celebrate."

I thought about the cake I'd had at book club, and how I'd talked with Ryan about it. Afterwards, I'd looked up a recipe for hummingbird cake and now I wanted to make it.

"My parents brought out champagne," I said, rolling my eyes.

"That is so cute, I love it," she said. My parents had met Sydney and loved her.

"They're too much sometimes," I said.

AFTER WORK, I stopped to get a few things from the grocery store. I grabbed some body wash and was just looking through the little selection of bath bombs when I felt someone behind me. I moved my cart so they could get around me, but they didn't. I looked up into a pair of stunning blue eyes.

"Ryan," I said. "What are you doing here?"

Ugh, I couldn't believe I'd said that. Obviously she was buying groceries at the grocery store.

To her credit, Ryan didn't make a sarcastic comment or anything, she just pointed to the basket she carried. I took a quick peek to see what she was buying.

"It's a small town, isn't it?" she said.

"Pretty much," I said, trying not to be too nosy. Looked like she had some steak and veggies and fruit and a few boxes of granola bars and one mini cake from the bakery.

"How's your week been so far?" I asked.

"So far, so good. I'm adjusting to not having so much to do and living without food delivery."

I laughed. "Yeah, that's a big one. You can't just call and order a pizza when you don't want to cook." Fortunately, I didn't do a lot of cooking, since my parents took care of it. I was pretty spoiled that way.

"I should let you get home, I'm sure you had a long day at work," she said, stepping back.

"Oh, yeah. I should get this ice cream home before it melts."

There was no ice cream in my cart, but she didn't need to know that.

"Good to see you again," she said.

"Wait," I said as she turned around. "You sure you don't want to spill something on me to even us up?"

Ryan gave me one of those flashes of a smile again. "Next time."

She headed toward the registers and I checked my list again and grabbed the last few items I needed. Ryan had already left, and I was wishing that we'd talked for longer. Time spent with her never felt like enough.

I'd had crushes in the past, and even a few relationships, but it had been a long time since I'd had these kinds of feelings about someone. When my anxiety had really gotten bad, it was like I'd shut off all these parts of me in service of survival. It's hard to think about dating when you can't even eat in a restaurant without having a panic attack.

With Ryan, those feelings were igniting again, and it was almost a relief. I'd thought that some of those parts of me might have died, or that I was unable to feel that way about someone again.

Of course, my crush had to be on the most completely unattainable woman in the history of women. Way to go, Everly.

THAT WEEKEND I didn't want to socialize, but I felt the need to get out of the house. Sometimes I liked to be around people, but not be with people. That was kind of hard to find in Arrowbridge, so since the weather was gorgeous, I headed down to the beach in Castleton. I loved that the ocean was so close to where I lived now, and it was a lot less intense than a beach in Massachusetts. My parents were going on an antiquing trip together, so I packed up my beach bag and chair in my car and headed out after breakfast for a day of sand and sun. No one gave you a weird look if you were by yourself at the beach, which was another good reason to go.

There was not a cloud in the perfectly blue sky as I parked my car and grabbed my stuff. I knew Layne and her group came here a lot, but I was hoping I wouldn't bump into anyone I knew. The energy just wasn't there for a whole lot of talking. I wanted to sit and read my book and take a quick dip and look for cool rocks to add to the collection on my windowsill. Ever since I was a kid, I always picked up interesting rocks and pebbles everywhere I'd gone. My parents loved to tell the story of me shoving rocks in my diaper and socks when I was little. More often than not I had one in my pocket and I would grab and hold onto it to help ground me when I was feeling anxious. Since I'd moved here, I'd found some excellent rocks in Castleton.

I huffed and puffed my way down the sand until I found an area that was further away from other people and set up my chair and towel. The sound of the waves was already so calming that I knew I'd made the right choice to come today.

I pulled out my bottle of ice water, my book, and set my phone on silent. Perfection.

∽

I SLIPPED INTO THE BOOK, a shorter novel about two former sports rivals who ended up in Cabo together with friends that Joy had recommended to me. The banter was great and it was really funny how competitive they were with each other. Halfway through I decided to stretch my legs and see just how cold the water was. Maine water was a whole lot colder than I was used to, that was for sure.

I pulled off the caftan I wore over my suit and folded it in my bag, which I clipped to and shoved under my chair.

"Shit, that's cold," I said as the waves rushed over my toes. I crept slowly in until I was up to my knees and wondered how there were people who just completely dove in and swam around like it was nothing. Not for me.

After I felt like I'd had enough of the water, I headed toward the edge of the beach, which was cluttered with shells and rocks and clumps of seaweed and other detritus.

I walked carefully over the stones, searching for anything that caught my eye. My favorites were always the ones that had a ring of color around them, known as wishing rocks. Mama had told me about them when I was little and ever since then, I tried to find as many as possible and make wishes on them.

The first rock I picked up wasn't right and I tossed it away after cleaning it with my fingers. A second rock also wasn't as pretty once I wiped away the sand.

Turned out third time was the charm as I found a dark gray rock with not one, but two unbroken white bands around it. Did that make it a double wishing rock?

"Find anything good?" a voice said, and I almost dropped the rock and slipped at the same time. Strong fingers helped me stay upright as I stared up into Ryan's face.

"We just keep ending up in the same place, don't we?" she said, and I nodded. As the shock of seeing her wore off, I noted her outfit. She wore a simple black swimsuit top under a thin tank and a pair of board shorts and leather sandals. Sparkly polish winked on her toenails, and it seemed out of step with the rest of her look.

"Nice toes," I couldn't stop myself from saying.

She wiggled them. "The twins got a hold of me."

I looked up into her face. "They can be very convincing," she added.

"It looks great," I said.

"You don't have to lie, Everly," she said.

"I'm not," I said.

There was something in the way she held herself that spoke of tension.

She gazed down the beach as the wind teased her hair and I did my best not to stare or ogle the abs that were visible through the thin tank. I'd been attracted to all kinds of women before, and right now those abs were speaking to me. Calling to me. Teasing me and making me want to touch.

"Are you having a nice day?" I asked.

"Mmm," she said. She appeared to have checked out of the conversation.

"I should, um, go check on my stuff," I said. If she didn't want to talk to me, and wasn't going to end this, then I wasn't going to stand here and feel awkward.

Ryan looked back at me, her eyes flicking up and down my body to take in my swimsuit. It was yellow with little leaf designs on it and ruffles on the bottoms.

"Have a good rest of your day," she said.

"Yeah, you too," I said and walked away.

Well, that was weird.

SINCE I'D SAID I was going back to my stuff, I had to go back, but at least I had one wishing stone. As soon as I sat back down, I looked back toward the end of the beach to search for Ryan. I didn't see her, so I scanned the sand for her blonde hair and distinctive frame.

My breath caught in my chest as I saw her pulling off her tank and setting her sunglasses on her blanket, which was closer to the other end of the beach than me, but I had a clear shot to watch her in between the other beachgoers.

Ryan walked toward the water with a confident stride and my mouth watered at the way she moved. What a body.

I'd never thought of myself as a shallow person, but I was lusting after Ryan Jewel, bottom line.

Sitting up in my seat, I watched as she took a few steps into the ocean and then dove under the waves with one smooth motion, as if she'd done it hundreds of times. In addition to polo, she'd probably had swimming lessons at least once in her life. Private swimming lessons in the large pool at her parent's house.

Ryan emerged and she slicked her hair back before starting to swim, as if she was doing laps. I didn't know much about swimming, but I knew good form when I saw it.

For a moment, I imagined throwing myself at the mercy of the ocean and having Ryan dramatically come to my rescue, those strong arms carrying me away from harm.

I looked down at my wishing stone and then back at Ryan as her arms sliced through the water with a practiced stroke.

"I want her," I said as I traced the edges of the stone. "I want Ryan Jewel."

Feeling foolish, I tossed the stone into my bag. Ridiculous.

I'D BROUGHT a sandwich for myself for lunch, but my entire body was craving french fries and ice cream, so I put my caftan on, grabbed my phone and my wallet, and headed to the snack bar.

There was a huge line, so I just scrolled my phone while I waited. By the time I made it to the order window, my stomach was growling. In addition to fries, my soul also called for a cheeseburger, so I ordered that too, with extra cheese. I got a little flustered ordering, but I made it through and went to wait for my order.

The cheeseburger and fries came out hot and my mouth watered as I added extra salt to the fries, along with a few shots of vinegar and took everything back to my chair. Honestly, I wished there were somewhere I could be with my cheeseburger privately as I shoved it in my mouth and almost moaned at how good it was. Cheese dripped down my chin and I was glad I'd grabbed enough napkins.

I looked around to make sure no one was staring at me having this moment with my cheeseburger, but everyone else at the beach was wrapped up in their own day. Mama always told me that when I was stressed about other people looking at me or judging me that they were all worried about me doing the same thing.

I was so hungry I had to tell myself to take small bites so I didn't choke. The fries were warm and salty and had the bite from the vinegar. The perfect combination.

Even though I was ready for a nap after all that, I had to go back and get my ice cream, a sundae with the works that I started eating as I walked back to my chair.

I went back to my book and then took another stroll up and down the beach after looking out for Ryan, but the spot where she'd been was occupied by different people. She must have finished her swim and left. I was trying not to be disappointed that I couldn't watch her anymore. Guess the wishing stone was a dud.

"YOU DEFINITELY GOT SOME SUN," Mama said when I came home that night, tired and sandy and a little crispy.

"I did my best," I said. Applying sunblock on your own wasn't easy, even with the spray kind.

"Let me get you some aloe lotion," Mama said, but I took her arm to stop her.

"I've got some in my bathroom, it's fine."

She frowned but didn't argue with me. Since I'd moved back in, both of my parents had been having issues with remembering that I was an adult and didn't require active parenting as much anymore. Yes, I needed some help and support when it came to my anxiety, but I didn't need her to fetch me lotion. I was more than capable of doing that myself.

"Did you have a good day?" she asked as I went to the laundry room to dump my towel.

"I did, it was exactly what I needed," I said.

She smiled and tucked some hair that had fallen from my messy bun over my ear.

"Good. Dinner will be ready in an hour if you want to go take a cool shower," she said.

"Sounds good."

I took my bag upstairs and went through it, finding the wishing stone. I rinsed it in the sink and then set it on the windowsill with the rest of my collection. I also had a few pieces of rare beach glass that I'd found over the years.

So many wishes all laid out together. Some had come true, others hadn't. I knew the one I'd made today wasn't going to come true, except in my dreams, where Ryan had been starring since the day we'd met.

My shower left me feeling drowsy, but there was also a competing sensation in my body that was a direct result of seeing Ryan in her swimsuit and imagining the rest of her body under it.

I'd never met anyone I'd wanted to literally bite before. Ryan Jewel was completely and totally biteable. And kissable. And fuckable.

I lay on my bed still in my towel as I licked my palm and then slipped it under to stroke myself. Sex was tricky for me with my anxiety, but I'd never had any issues with masturbation, which was a relief. I'd even used it as a coping mechanism for a time when my anxiety had gotten really bad. That was one of the things that first drove me to therapy, and since then, I'd managed to have more normal self-love habits.

Within seconds, I was wet and sliding two fingers inside, adjusting my hips so the angle was right. My eyes shut so I could fully throw myself into the fantasy playing out in my mind. Ryan. Her hands and mouth everywhere on my body, her smile seductive and a little devious. Those fingers tugging at my nipples, stroking down my stomach, plunging inside me and touching me just right. She'd know exactly what I wanted, what I needed. Her mouth would be relentless first on mine, and then lower, where she'd use her tongue on me.

I gasped as I got close to falling over the edge and pinched my nipple with my left hand, sending a bolt of feeling right between my legs. A few more thrusts of my fingers followed by stroking the side of my clit and I was done. My breath gasped out as I surrendered, jerking and tingling with pleasure.

I let out a little sigh and sat up, feeling warm and glowy.

"Dinner's ready!" Mom called up the stairs.

～

"I CAN'T BELIEVE I'm not on vacation anymore," Sydney said on Monday as we opened the shop. "Is there a term for the sadness you feel at returning to your life after going on vacation?"

"I'm sure there is in German," I said.

She laughed. "True. Did you do anything fun this weekend?"

"Went to the beach on Saturday. It was so nice."

"I'm jealous. Lark and I didn't do much of anything besides laundry and cleaning and dealing with all the crap we didn't deal with while we were gone." She made a face. "Anyway, enough complaining. Sorry, didn't mean to be a black cloud."

"It's okay," I said. I couldn't remember the last time I'd gone on any kind of trip or vacation. Helping my parents move by driving a truck from Massachusetts didn't count.

"Are you doing anything this week? Lark has been learning to cook from Layne and she wants to try and make this fancy chicken thing and I think she wants more guinea pigs to try it on than just me."

"Oh," I said, my brain already scrambling for excuses. "It'll be just you and Lark?"

"Joy and Ezra are coming too. It's not exactly a dinner party, because we're not fancy like that, but we will be eating dinner in a casual setting," she said. "You don't have to answer right now. Just let me know."

A few customers walked in and I was saved from having to answer.

It sounded lowkey, so I was going to try for it. When it came to my anxiety, I never took anything for granted. Just when I'd get cocky and think that I had it conquered, a random panic attack would slam me back to earth.

Sydney had the front of the shop covered, so I went to the back to pack orders. Since she'd hired me, Sydney had expanded the offerings in the online shop, and had reached out to more places to sell mugs and coasters and other things on consignment. A few times a month I would go around to the shops and refresh the inventory and see how everything was selling. The first few times I'd done it had been a nightmare, but I was much better at it now.

There was something about packing boxes that was so soothing, and I never minded doing it.

Eileen had her earbuds in, probably listening to some podcast, so I put on an audiobook to keep me company while I worked, going to the computer to print off the shipping labels, pulling the merchandise, and then making sure it was all cozy and wrapped up tight so it wouldn't break in transit.

I got into the groove and my book was getting steamy. Compared to the other jobs that were available locally, this one was pretty close to perfect.

The rest of the day passed quickly, in between packing and heading to the post office, I helped Eileen clean up a container of glaze she spilled and helped Sydney with some website updates.

"I'll come to your not dinner party," I told her as we were closing up the shop for the day.

"Fantastic. I think it's going to be on Wednesday, but I'll let you know so you can plan. It'll be super casual, so you don't need to bring anything or wear anything fancy. Just dinner with friends," she said.

Dinner with friends. I could handle that. I hoped.

WHILE I DIDN'T SEE or hear anything about Ryan the next two days, she was constantly in my thoughts. I knew so little about her that I had nothing but questions. Where was she staying? What did she do with her days? Did she have a job? I didn't even know how old she was. Older than me, but by how much?

Ryan Jewel was a mystery I didn't think I would get a chance to solve.

Chapter Five

THE DINNER PARTY was actually moved to Thursday night. I only worked a half day, since I was helping that weekend. Due to not having much of a social life, I didn't mind having to work weekends sometimes.

Thursday afternoon I tried to stay busy, running errands and cleaning my room, having a therapy session, and doing whatever I could not to ruminate too much on what was happening later.

Both my parents were at work, so it was really nice to have the house to myself for a few hours during the week. They came home as I was getting ready, sliding into a pair of jeans and a comfy T-shirt.

"Look at you, our little social butterfly," Mama said when I grabbed my bag and said I was heading out.

"I wouldn't go that far. I don't think I'll ever stop being a wallflower, but I'm okay with that," I said. Walls were sturdy and sometimes formed corners to hide in. I was a big fan of walls.

I parked in the lot behind the pottery shop, which was also

Surprised By Her

the lot for Sydney's apartment, since it was upstairs in the same building, but with a separate back entrance.

I knocked on the door and heard someone call that it was open, and to beware of the cat. I turned the knob and immediately Sydney's fluffy orange cat, Clementine, rushed over to inspect me. I leaned down to rub his sweet head as he purred against me.

Sometimes I thought about getting a pet as a distraction from my anxiety, but I didn't know if I'd want to leave it during the day. That might make me even more anxious in the end.

"Hey, thanks for coming," Lark said, coming over to say hello. She had blonde curly hair and it was obvious she was Honor's sister, but Honor's way more chill sister.

"Yeah, thanks for inviting me," I said, slipping out of my shoes and adding them to the pile near the door.

The apartment was small, and it was feeling a lot smaller due to how many people were inside. It wasn't just Sydney, Lark, Joy, and Ezra. Layne and Honor were here as well, and Lark's redheaded friend from work, Mia, and one other person who seemed to take up half the living room on her own.

Sydney must have seen the panic on my face and came over.

"Hey, so sorry about this," she said in a low voice, herding me toward the kitchen area. "I didn't mean for this many people to come, but it just kind of happened. If you want to bail, I can make up a good excuse."

I felt myself starting to sweat and tremble a little but leaving would only cause more embarrassing questions than sucking it up and staying. I could keep it together.

The noise level was already grating on me, but I'd just gotten here. I'd get used to it.

"It's okay," I said. "I'm okay, I can handle this."

"You sure?" Sydney asked.

I nodded. "Yeah. I'll send you a 911 if I need to bail."

"Don't hesitate. Also, if you need to take a breather, you can use the library," she said. She and Lark had moved into the room that was formerly Sydney's, and they used Lark's old room as a place to store their books and extra clothes. They had a sweet little daybed in there in case they ever had a guest. As far as places to have a panic attack, it was pretty nice.

"Thanks," I said. "That helps a lot."

"Sorry, I have to get to the oven," Lark said, so Sydney and I moved toward the packed living room. I said hello to everyone, and Joy asked me if I wanted a drink. The temptation to get wasted was strong, but I asked for a soda instead.

Ryan stood in a corner with Layne and Honor, who seemed to be deep in discussion about something.

I met her eyes and she said something to Layne and Honor and came over to me.

"I guess it's true what they say about small towns," she said.

"It is," I said immediately, but then wasn't quite sure what she meant. "Wait, what is it they say about small towns?"

"Small towns, small world. You're bound to see the same people," she said.

"Here you go my dear," Joy said, bringing me my soda. "Ryan, can I get you a refill?"

"No, thank you, I'm fine," Ryan said, and Joy moved on. I guess she had taken it upon herself to be the bartender tonight, even though it wasn't her party and she didn't live here anymore.

I was about to say something else to Ryan, but then I heard someone tapping silverware against a glass and calling for everyone's attention.

Lark cleared her throat. "Dinner is ready so…come and get it."

We all lined up and grabbed plates and served ourselves from the pans and dishes in the kitchen.

Sydney had brought up a folding table from the pottery

shop and found some folding chairs somewhere. It was a tight squeeze, but we managed to all fit without an inch to spare.

I wound up at the end of the table with Sydney on my right and Ryan on my left. Not sure if she intended to sit next to me, but that's how it happened and then I was practically pressed up against her as she wedged herself into her chair.

"Sorry," I said, trying to give her as much space as possible.

"You're fine," Ryan said, adjusting her chair. No matter what she did, most of her body was practically pressed up against mine and my brain was starting to short-circuit at all the contact.

Ryan was tall and warm, and she smelled so good. Even better than the food in front of me.

"I'd like to make a toast," Layne said, piping up. "I want to say thank you to Lark for this incredible meal, and to Sydney for hosting. Cheers everyone," she said, and we all toasted.

"Cheers," Ryan said softly as our glasses met for a brief touch. I forced myself to meet her eyes, since I knew that if you didn't make eye contact during a toast, you were doomed to years of bad luck. Not that I believed in that, but it was better safe than sorry.

Ryan did her best, but she was constantly bumping into me as she tried to eat. I knew I should move over or at least lean a little to give her more room, but every time our bodies collided, it gave me a little thrill.

"Love, this is amazing," Sydney said, looking down the end of the table toward Lark. "And I'm not just saying that to get into your pants later. It *is* something I'd say to get into your pants, but in this instance, it's not a lie."

Lark snorted. "Thank you, Syd. That's very nice to hear."

I couldn't even concentrate on the food because of Ryan. She was a hell of a distraction from my anxiety.

At one point her thigh rubbed against mine and I dropped my fork.

"Sorry," she said under her breath.

"It's okay," I said, picking my fork up again. At least it hadn't fallen on the floor.

Clementine the cat made his rounds, trying to see if any tasty tidbits would fall on the floor for him to gobble up. He actually jumped into Sydney's lap and tried to paw at her plate.

"Sir, this is not for you. This is human food and you hate all of it. I know what you like and there's none of it here." The cat blinked up at her and meowed before she set him on the floor again.

The longer we sat at the table, the more tense Ryan seemed to get until her entire body was in one huge clench. I felt bad for her and was relieved when everyone finished and we could leave the table. Lark had bought dessert from Sweet's Sweets and went to the kitchen with Sydney to brew coffee and tea for everyone.

Others rose from the table with their plates to help clean up, and I stood to give Ryan some room. I swore I heard her sigh in relief as she stood and stretched her arms over her head, her shirt riding up a little to give me a tiny peek of those abs I'd seen at the beach. I forgot everything I was doing for a moment until someone said something to me.

"Huh?" I said, turning away from Ryan.

"Coffee or tea for you?" Joy asked.

"Oh, uh, tea, please. Herbal." If I had caffeine now, I was never going to get to sleep.

"Sure thing," Joy said. "Ryan?"

"Coffee. Black," she said.

"Coming right up," Joy said, moving on to taking other orders.

I started feeling like I was hitting my social limit and needed a break. The noise of everyone talking and the effort it took to converse and keep a smile on my face and come up with responses had worn me out, so I headed to the guest room slash library to have some space. No one said anything to me, and I let out a breath of relief as I closed the door, muffling the sound.

Sydney and Lark had quite the book collection between them, so I browsed the titles, pulling any out that intrigued me so I could remind myself to add them to my to-buy list when I got my next paycheck.

My body slowly came down and started to reset itself. I sat on the bed and pulled up a book on my phone to read until I was ready to join the party again. I'd just read the first paragraph when there was a soft knock at the door.

"Come in?" I said, hoping it was just Sydney checking on me.

It wasn't Sydney that walked through the doorway. It was Ryan.

"Oh," I said.

"Sorry to disturb you," she said in a low voice as she shut the door behind her.

"It's okay," I said as she filled the room.

"It was getting crowded out there," she said.

"I know. Their apartment isn't exactly made for entertaining," I said.

"No," she said. "I didn't expect it to be so many people."

"Me neither," I said. "I needed a break."

She nodded and I watched her eyes flick over the bookshelves, looking at the spines of the books.

"I'm not disturbing you, am I?" she asked.

"No," I said. "You're fine."

She nodded and lapsed into silence. Something about her energy communicated that she didn't want to chat. Ryan had never given me the impression she was a chatter, but especially now she appeared to crave silence.

That was fine with me. She paced the room and started

looking closer at the bookshelves, and I pretended to go back to reading.

In reality, I was ogling her. A whole lot easier to do when her back was turned to me.

What a beautiful back it was. I longed to touch her, to trace those muscles beneath her shirt. My gaze traveled lower, to the perfect roundness of her ass. So very biteable.

There was another knock at the door that made me look up with guilt, even though no one had caught me doing anything.

Sydney poked her head in.

"Hey, just wanted to check on you and make sure you didn't want any dessert."

Right. Dessert.

"Of course," Ryan said without looking at me. She left the room without a backwards glance and I followed her back into the living room.

∼

DESSERT WAS NICE, but soon it was time for me to head home. Ryan didn't say anything else to me, and I hoped I hadn't said anything that upset her, or said something wrong. I didn't get a chance to ask, since she had slipped out when I'd been in the bathroom.

So much for that.

I thanked Sydney and Lark and walked down to my car, still thinking about Ryan.

I couldn't get a read on her, and it was both frustrating and intriguing. A closed book that I wished to open and read the pages of.

Chapter Six

"So, what were you and Ryan chatting about in the library last night?" Sydney slyly asked me the next day during a lull. The shop had been busy all day, so I'd been out helping Sydney with the customers and I'd been glad for the break.

"Nothing, actually. I just needed a breather and I guess she did too. She didn't have any room at the table," I said.

Sydney made a face. "Yeah, that was a mistake. We should have gotten another table or had people sit on the couch. I apologized to her a bunch of times."

"I think she knew it wasn't your fault," I said.

"I hope so. She doesn't really give you a lot when you talk to her," she said. Finally, some information on Ryan. I was trying not to look too eager.

"What's her story anyway?" I asked, hoping my voice sounded uninterested.

"You don't know? She's an heiress."

I snorted. "Okay."

"No, for real." Sydney pulled something up on her phone. It was a picture taken from an event by press of a tall man, a tall woman, and their tall daughter.

"That's her," I said, stating the obvious. Ryan looked like a perfect combination of her parents, and she'd come by her height honestly. Her mother was stunning, and her father had a regal air about him.

Sydney had left me with her phone to go grab something and she came back with a candle we used as part of a display.

"Her family makes these," she said, holding it up. The candle was a brand you saw everywhere, including entire stores you'd find in a mall.

"Wait, her family makes those?" I said, pointing to the candle.

"I mean, they don't literally make them, but they own the company, yeah. That's why she doesn't have to work. Maybe she'll take over the company one day, but right now she's free as a bird. A super rich bird." Sydney showed me the house, I mean mansion, where Ryan had grown up and my eyes went so wide I thought they were going to fall out of my head. Ryan hadn't just played polo. Her family own an entire horse farm and had owned at least one horse that had run in the Kentucky Derby.

My stomach sank. Ryan was in a whole other stratosphere of life.

"It was weird inviting her to my apartment, seeing as how she could probably buy all of the buildings on Main Street with cash and not blink an eye," Sydney said.

"Wow," I said, at a loss for any other words.

"Yeah, seriously. Layne told me and my jaw dropped to the floor. Let me tell you, I've never cleaned my bathroom like that before." She laughed and shook her head.

"Wow," I said again.

"Anyway, I assume that level of wealth makes you a little aloof, so that kind of explains her whole deal. I'm sure she's used to people finding out she's rich and then not being sure if they're going to pump her for money or not," Sydney said, and my response was interrupted by some of our regular customers walking into the shop. They'd come for free coffee and gossip and to see what was new. Sydney turned up the charm, but I was still thinking about what I'd just learned about Ryan.

It made sense that Ryan would be wary of people she didn't know, but it had to be more than that for her. She reminded me a little bit of Ezra. They both held themselves away from others. Ezra's wariness with others was due to family strife, Joy had told me. But what made Ryan tick? What were the ingredients that had come together to make her the person she was?

Much to think about.

~

"ARE you going to a party this weekend?" Mama asked me on Friday night. Mom had stopped at Nick's Pizza and brought back pizza, salad, and garlic knots for us.

"Not that I know of," I said, dipping another garlic knot in marinara. Tonight we were cozy on the couch with TV trays to hold everything instead of at the dining table.

"No?" Mom asked.

"No," I said. "Why?"

They shared a glance. "We just thought you were getting out more," Mama finally said.

"I literally went to a party last night," I said. That had been more than enough socializing for the week.

"Oh, well," Mama said, going for another slice of pizza.

"What?" I asked.

"It just seemed like you had some momentum that might lead to other things," Mom said.

"I have momentum," I said, feeling defensive. "I told you, I hung out with people last night."

"You know, you could always invite some of your friends

over here. We'll make ourselves scarce. You could have a sleepover!" Mama said.

"Mama, I'm not twelve. If I'm having a sleepover, I'm going to rent a hotel or something." The other reason I'd have a sleepover is if I was dating someone, but that was a completely different thing and I didn't want to discuss those details with my parents at the moment.

"We just want you to feel free to invite anyone over," Mom said. "If you wanted to."

"I'll let you know," I said, licking garlic butter off my fingers.

SATURDAY I SLEPT in and woke to rain pattering on the windows. I watched the water sliding down the glass for a few moments before I got up. I had to work until noon and then I had the rest of the weekend for myself. Right now, my plans included curling up in my favorite chair in the corner of the living room and reading as much as I possibly could with a plate of snacks. I might put a record on my parent's turntable to really set the ambience. The perfect weekend.

Work flew by with the shop packed with customers from the minute I unlocked the door to when I told the last customers that I needed to close and that we'd be open for a few hours on Sunday and they could come back.

It was still raining, much to my delight, and the bookstore was open until four, so I headed down the street and ducked into the shop, shaking off my umbrella. The bookstore was also busy, so I had to shove myself in between other customers to browse.

Joy wasn't working today, but Kendra, the owner, and Erin were, but I knew they probably had their hands full. It was up to me to figure out what to read.

I hit the queer romance area, with the new releases on the top shelf. There were two new sapphic romances I hadn't read, so I grabbed them before I decided to scan the historical romances and then the nonfiction. I was a big fan of biographies of interesting people. My last stops were the craft books and crossword puzzles for my parents, but nothing new there.

I got in line and pulled out my phone to amuse myself while I waited. From what I could overhear, there was a problem with the card swiper, so poor Erin was completely frazzled. I hoped people were being kind to her.

"Find anything interesting?" a voice said, and I looked over my shoulder right into a familiar chest. I raised my eye level so I didn't seem like a creep. She did have a lovely chest, though.

"Hey," I said. "I did." I held the books up so she could see.

"Did you get anything?" I asked.

She held up our next book club pick, a wildly popular cozy fantasy book about an orc opening a coffee shop. I was really excited about reading and discussing it, but I hadn't started yet.

"Nice," I said. "I was hoping we'd read that one."

Ryan looked down at the book and nodded. Guess we were done chatting.

The line moved forward as I tried to think of something else to say.

"I love rainy weekend days. They make me feel so cozy," I blurted out.

Ryan nodded. "I agree."

At last, it was time for me to pay and I said hello to Erin, who looked tired.

"I think we're back up and running, but let's cross our fingers things don't go down again," she said as I prepared to pay with my card. I knocked on the wooden counter as she added a bookmark in between one of the covers.

The card went through and she handed me the receipt as I stuffed the books in my bag to protect them from the rain.

"Enjoy the book," I told Ryan as she stepped up to the counter.

"You too," she said.

I bit my lip, knowing I should leave, but always feeling that tug of something unsaid between us.

"Have a nice weekend, Ryan," I finally said.

She nodded and turned back to Erin.

~

MOM WAS WATCHING sports and Mama was baking a cake when I got home. I went to the kitchen to make myself a snack plate and chat with Mama before heading to my favorite chair in Mama's office to read the day away.

I wondered if Ryan was doing the same thing with her new book. I hoped she liked it.

I opened the cover of the first book I wanted to read and closed it a few seconds later. I grabbed my phone instead, looking up Ryan Jewel online. Mostly what I found were articles about her father with her name mentioned. She did have some social media accounts, but they were all set to private, and I wasn't going to request to follow her. Disappointed, I set my phone aside and went back to my book.

~

LAYNE STOPPED in to visit with Sydney on Monday afternoon.

"The girls are down the street at the boutique. They've helped out for years, but now since they're older Sadie has given them more responsibility," she said. The Rizo clothing boutique was a bit out of my price range, but they did have really nice clothes. When I saved up a little more money I might stop in to update my wardrobe. Everything I currently owned came from thrift stores or big box discount stores.

"That's good. Put 'em to work," Sydney said. "They should learn now that nothing comes for free."

"Isn't that the truth?" Layne said, and then turned to me. "Hey, Everly, I also came in to ask you a favor."

"Me?" I asked. What could she need from me?

"Yeah, I've seen you talking to Ryan a few times, and I was wondering if maybe you could ask her if she wants to hang out."

"Me?" I repeated.

Layne nodded. "Yeah. She doesn't really open up to...well, anyone, and she's been kind of holed up in her rental unless I drag her out or she goes for a swim by herself at the beach. She'll hang out with the twins, but I'm trying to get her to come out of her shell and talk with other adults and hoped you might want to help?"

It was a strange request, but not out of step with what I knew about Layne. "She wants to fix everyone," Sydney told me before I met her the first time. I guess Ryan wasn't immune from that urge.

"Oh, I don't know..." I said, trailing off. Wouldn't Ryan see right through me if I did that?

"Just think about it," Layne said, holding up one hand. "She's had a rough time of it lately."

Had she? I tried not to lean forward too much with interest.

Layne sighed. "Yeah, there was a breakup and then her ex got married like three months later to one of their mutual friends. But I didn't tell you that." She pointed at me with emphasis.

"Tell me what?" I asked.

Layne grinned. "Exactly."

"Layne, do you really think setting Ryan up on a friend

date is what you need to be doing? What does Honor think about that?"

Layne snorted. "She told me to stop meddling, but she tells me that about everything."

Sydney gave Layne a look.

"If people would just do what I think they should, then I wouldn't have to meddle," Layne said.

Sydney laughed. "I guess you're right."

They fell back into conversation about other things while I went into the back to pack orders and think about what Layne had asked me to do. First of all, how would I even approach Ryan about this? I didn't have her number, didn't know where she lived, had had no contact with her other than running into her.

Right then, I made a deal with myself. If I somehow bumped into Ryan in the next two days, then I had to ask her to hang out. That way, it was out of my hands.

I HAD to stop at the convenience store just outside of Arrowbridge after work to pick up some deodorant, face wash, and some candy as a little gift for my parents. I was choosing between two candy bar options for myself when I felt someone standing behind me.

"Can't decide?" the person said, just as a wave of familiar scent hit my nose.

"Ryan," I said as I turned around. It hadn't even been four hours since I'd seen Layne. "At this point, I'm going to have to ask if you're stalking me."

She reached for some mints and shook her head.

"I'm not. There are only so many places to go in this small town," she said.

"You sound like that's a bad thing," I said.

"I like having more options," she said.

"Arrowbridge has plenty of options," I said, feeling a little defensive of my adopted town.

"Does it?"

"Yes," I said.

She arched one perfect eyebrow. I bet she got microblading. No one was born with brows like that. Or maybe she got them groomed in some rich people way that the rest of the world didn't even know about.

"Name five restaurants in Arrowbridge," she said.

I narrowed my eyes. "There aren't five restaurants in Arrowbridge."

"Exactly."

I let out a breath. "We don't need a bunch of restaurants when we have Nick's."

"Don't they just serve pizza? It's called 'Nick's Pizza'."

"That's what you think," I said. "Nick's has pizza, an entire Greek food menu, and they serve breakfast."

Ryan's immaculate brows contracted. "That's confusing."

"It's clever. One restaurant covering several food bases. Where else can you order mozzarella sticks, pancakes, and spanakopita at the same time?" I asked.

Ryan pulled out her phone and typed something before presenting me with the screen.

"These places," she said.

I looked from the phone to her face. "You like being right, don't you?"

"Only when I'm right, which is most of the time."

This was the most she'd talked to me since the time in the guest room and I couldn't stop the giddy feeling from spreading in my chest. Being around Ryan made me feel...like that first big drop of a roller coaster. Thrilling and out of control and wonderful and too much all at the same time.

"Well, if you like options so much, why aren't you eating from Nick's?" I asked.

"I didn't know about all the cuisine options until now," she said. "Now I'll have to go."

"You should," I said, and I realized she had given me the perfect opportunity to do what Layne asked.

"You might need some help, you know. Someone who knows what to order," I said. "I'm very experienced with dining at Nick's." I had never felt suave or confident in my entire life, but I think I was giving some approximation of it.

"Are you?" she said.

"I am," I said. "So, if you're not doing anything, say, Friday night, I'd be happy to make some room in my schedule for you."

Who the hell was I right now? Where was this coming from? I had no idea, but I was going to go with it.

Ryan let out an unmistakable laugh. It rumbled through her chest and made my body temperature go up a few degrees.

"It's a deal. How about I pick you up around seven?" she said.

Oh. I hadn't counted on that. I assumed she'd just drive herself and I could walk over after work.

"Um, yeah, sure," I said.

"What's your number?" she asked, and I gave it to her. My phone buzzed with a message from her a moment later.

"There. Now you can send me your address." She absolutely could have gotten both my number and my address from Layne, but she'd decided to do it this way and I didn't know why.

She reached behind me and plucked a candy bar from the display.

"See you tomorrow," she said.

"See you," I said, leaning on the display for support.

Chapter Seven

"A friend is picking me up to go to dinner tomorrow night," I said when I was eating with my parents.

"A friend?" Mama said, her eyes bright with excitement.

"Yeah, she's, um, staying here for the summer and Layne asked me to help her get out of the house," I said. I'd practiced what I was going to say on the way home from the store.

"That's nice of you," Mom said. "Does she have social anxiety too?"

"No, she's just new in town."

"Is it Ryan Jewel?" Mama said.

"How do you know about Ryan Jewel?" I asked.

"Just about everyone has been talking about her," Mama said. "You have no idea how many people want to see if they can sell her a house here and make a commission."

That made sense.

"Well, it's her. She's Mark's—Layne's boss—niece, so Layne has known her forever. I'm not really sure why she singled me out to talk to her," I said.

"You're a kind person with a good spirit," Mama said, as if it was the most obvious thing in the world.

"Remember when you used to volunteer at the animal shelter? You were the only one who could work with the most hopeless cases," Mom said. In high school I used to volunteer at the local animal shelter, both for my college applications and because I loved doing it. I guess I'd been kind of drawn to the animals that needed a little bit of extra love.

"I guess," I said.

"Can you do one thing for me?" Mama asked.

"Sure," I said.

"Can you ask her why they discontinued the Fall Frolic candle two years ago? It was my favorite. Oh, and ask her if she has access to any. I'm willing to pay," she said.

"I'm not asking her for candles, Mama," I said.

"Just work it into the conversation. I really miss the scent of that candle," she said.

"I'll see what I can do."

LATER THAT NIGHT I sent Ryan my address.

See you tomorrow she replied.

I couldn't help but be a little disappointed by her simple response, but maybe she didn't want to talk.

Sighing, I set my phone down and went to take a shower. When I came back to my phone, I had a notification.

I know Layne told you to hang out with me, just so we have everything on the table she sent.

Shit.

I'm sorry. I told myself I'd only do it if I ran into you and then we were talking about Nick's and it just sort of came out. I understand if you don't want to go now I hurriedly typed out, the panic rising inside me.

She started responding, then stopped, then tried again.

If it wasn't you, it would have been someone else.

Layne is a force of nature. I'm used to her by now. Sorry you got roped in she sent.

I'm really sorry I responded.

Everly. I'm not angry with you. I'll pick you up at seven tomorrow she replied.

There was something about the tone that reassured me. Although my thoughts were still telling me that she was upset with me, that she was just placating me for now, her words did give me some comfort.

I had no idea how this was going to turn out.

I KIND OF ASSUMED THAT Ryan would tell Layne about our little pizza outing, so I didn't feel obligated to say anything, but Sydney knew that something was up with me the next day, so I broke down and confessed.

"We're going for pizza at Nick's," I said. "She hasn't been there, so I wanted to introduce her to what Arrowbridge has to offer."

"It's not much," Sydney said with a snort. She'd grown up here, so I understood that she might be tired of everything in this town. "Nick's is really good, though. It's nice of you to do."

It rubbed me the wrong way that both Layne and Sydney were acting like hanging out with Ryan was some act of charity. Had they seen her? Getting pizza with an incredibly hot woman was not a hardship for me. Even if they didn't know about the kiss, it was still weird.

I shrugged one shoulder. "I like talking to her."

Sydney seemed shocked by that. "I don't think I've ever gotten more than a few words out of her. Eventually I just kind of stopped trying, and I'm a goddamn delight to talk to."

Sydney, while she was a delight, could be a lot to take. I

could handle her, but not everyone could. She also had a tendency to dominate a conversation.

"Maybe she's just not intimidated by me." It was one of my many annoyances with myself. People always thought I was much younger than my age. Hell, I was probably going to get carded until I was forty. I was twenty-six and strangers would mistake me for a high school student. There's nothing intimidating about that.

"Maybe she just likes you," Sydney said offhand.

I scoffed. "I don't think so."

That kiss was definitely an anomaly, seeing as how she hadn't tried to do it again, and had acted like she wanted to pretend it never even happened.

"I know Joy is the romantic one who's always shipping people, but I think I saw something between you two. Just… \keep your eyes open."

I looked at her and deliberately widened my eyes.

"Maybe tone it down just a little before you see her," she said.

"Noted," I said.

AS THE EVENING APPROACHED, I got more and more jittery about getting pizza with Ryan. It wasn't even a date or anything close to a date, and I was practically vibrating out of my skin. My normal anxiety was high, but it was fighting with the butterflies that had taken up residence in my stomach since last night. There was a lot going on in my body and it almost made me want to send her a message and cancel. I almost did so at least a dozen times, including while I was getting ready. My body was so exhausted from anxiety that all I wanted to do was crawl into my bed with a book and not talk to have to interact with anyone for at least a day.

Instead, I picked out my clothes, going for casual with a wide-leg pant and a white T-shirt. I put in silver earrings my mom had gotten me for my birthday and checked the rest of the hoops in my right ear. I had a total of eight piercings, all in my ears, with seven in one ear. When I'd come home with a bunch of holes in my ear, my parents had said at least they weren't tattoos. I'd wanted to get tattoos, but could never think of a good one that I'd want to have for a long time. Piercing my ears was quick and fun and pretty low on the pain scale, but still made me feel like I was doing something.

After one last check to make sure my underwear wasn't visible, I headed downstairs to wait for Ryan to pick me up, sitting in my favorite chair—which also had a convenient view of the driveway so I could see her coming down the road.

At exactly five minutes before seven, a pair of headlights came down the road and turned into the driveway. The outside light came on, illuminating the fanciest car I'd ever seen in in Arrowbridge. Sure, there were a few rich people who had homes here, but a lot of them had undercover wealth and drove nice cars, but not luxury cars. Honor was the only person I knew who had something even close to that.

Ryan's car was on a whole other level.

My breath caught in my throat as she got out and walked up the porch. I made sure to hide behind the curtains so she couldn't see me watching her.

She knocked decisively on the door.

"Bye, I'll be back later!" I called to my parents and went to open the door.

"Hi," I said, sounding breathless.

"Hello," Ryan said. "Ready to go?"

"Yup," I said as I heard my parents coming down the hall. "Let's go. Now."

I tried to shove Ryan out of the way so we didn't have an

awkward encounter with my parents, but it was like trying to move a brick wall.

"Everly?" Mama said.

"Go, go go," I said to Ryan, rushing down the steps and speaking over my shoulder "love you, bye!"

I threw myself in the passenger seat and Ryan got in the driver's seat with less speed than I would have liked. My parents stood in the doorway with puzzled looks on their faces.

"Please go," I said, and she put the car in reverse and backed out before turning onto the main road. I waved at my parents as we sped away.

"Anything I need to know about? Are you escaping from something?" she said as the car purred down the pothole-studded road.

"My parents are…they're great, but I didn't want to unleash them on you right yet. They can be a bit much." If I'd let them, they would have dragged Ryan inside and bombarded her with questions and maybe even held her hostage.

"You're close with them," she said, not as a question.

"Always have been, even when I didn't live with them. They're amazing."

Ryan didn't say anything for a little while.

"This is a really nice car," I said, my body sinking into the leather seats.

"Thank you," she said. "I'm thinking of getting rid of it."

"Oh? What would you get instead?" I asked.

"I'm open to suggestions," she said.

"I don't know much about cars." Mine was one I'd inherited from Mama when she upgraded after closing a huge sale and making a big commission. In fact, all of the cars I'd ever owned had been hand-me-downs, so I'd never even shopped for one, unless you counted going with my parents when they bought one.

"I'd still like to hear your opinion," she said, and I looked at her in surprise. She wanted to know my opinion? I felt my cheeks turn red and was grateful she had her eyes on the road.

"I have to think about this for a little bit," I said.

"Take your time."

I didn't say anything until she pulled into the parking lot next to Nick's.

Ryan turned the car off and faced me. "Well?"

"I'm still thinking," I said. "While this car is very nice, it's not…you. I picture you in something older. Classic. Red, maybe black. Sleek, but aggressive. The kind of car that people would compliment you on. A car that required a little bit of elbow grease to keep it running," I said, and I couldn't read the expression on her face. I'd never met someone so good at hiding their emotions before. She should teach classes.

"How did I do?" I asked when she didn't say anything for a few seconds.

"It sounds like a midlife crisis car," she said, as if she was fighting a smile.

"You're too young for a midlife crisis," I said.

She raised one eyebrow. "I'm thirty-eight."

"Oh," I said. She didn't look thirty-eight, but I'd never been a good judge of people's ages. "That's still not middle aged."

"What is middle age?"

"At *least* forty-five," I said.

That made her laugh. "Come on, I'm hungry."

I GOT A BETTER LOOK at her outfit when we walked into Nick's and got in line. She wore black joggers and a gray T-shirt that was thin and tight, not leaving much to my imagination. Casual, but sexy.

"I didn't get a chance to say so earlier, but you look really nice," she said.

"Thanks. So do you," I said, blushing again.

Nick's was packed, and I didn't know where the hell we were going to sit.

"It's probably a fifteen-minute wait," a server said to us on the way to drop off a few plates.

"We don't have to eat here," I said. "We could get it to go and take it somewhere else."

"That works," she said, and I snagged us some menus.

"This is a novel," Ryan said, turning the pages.

"What are you in the mood for? The eggplant parmesan is superb, as is the spinach and artichoke pizza. My parents get the everything pizza, which is good too. Or if you're in the mood for something else, the seasonal salad is massive," I said.

"Chicken pot pie pizza?" Ryan said, her voice skeptical.

"That one's better when it's cold," I said, and she shook her head.

"I think I'll take your word for it on that one. What are you going to get?" she asked.

The line moved as Nick efficiently took orders, yelling back to his husband Tony, who was in charge of the kitchen.

"I'm feeling the barbecue chicken tonight with a side salad. How do you feel about cheeseburger sliders as an appetizer?" I asked her.

"Sounds delicious," she said.

We finally got up to order and Ryan smoothly told Nick that our orders were together, leaving no room for me to protest as she continued to speak, ordering the everything pizza.

"Just so you know, it's so weighted down with toppings, you have to eat it with a fork," I told her.

"Noted," she said.

We stepped aside to wait for our order and Ryan leaned

against the wall her gaze flicking around the room, as if she was taking everything in.

"I know your secret," I said. She gave me her full attention, turning her whole body toward me.

"What secret is that?" she asked, crossing her arms. Momentarily stunned by those arms, it took me a second to remember what I'd been about to say.

"Sydney told me who you are. Who your family is," I said.

She raised her eyebrows. "And?"

"And I know. I guess that's it." Why had I brought this up? Now I'd just made things awkward.

"That's it?" she asked.

"Yeah. I know you weren't like, hiding it or anything, but I figured you'd probably wanted to keep it quiet here," I said, moving closer to her as a family with at least five kids stepped over to wait for a table.

Ryan studied me for a few moments in silence.

"I wasn't trying to keep it quiet. I just…didn't want to talk about it," she said.

"That's fine, you don't have to. But if you wanted to, you could talk to me." Not that I knew anything about the pressures of being a candle heiress, but I knew how to listen.

"I'll keep that in mind," she said, her arms relaxing a little.

"The place I think we should eat our pizza isn't technically in Arrowbridge, but it's well worth a drive down the road," I said.

"Is it?"

I nodded and two of the kids crashed into my legs as they chased each other around and I fell into Ryan's chest. If her reflexes hadn't been so good, I would have face-planted right into her tits. I wouldn't have minded one bit, but she probably would have.

"Sorry," I gasped, but she didn't let go of me right away. Her fingers twitched, digging into my skin for a fraction of a heartbeat before she basically picked me up and set me on my feet again.

Nick called for our order and Ryan went to fetch it.

"Lead the way," she said to me as she carried everything.

"OKAY, TURN RIGHT HERE," I told her.

"If you weren't so tiny, I might be worried for my safety," she said.

"Hey, I can be dangerous. You don't know," I said. "I could be really good with knives. Or poisons."

Ryan looked at me out of the corner of her eye. "I think I can take you."

"Oh, turn here," I said.

Ryan pulled into the parking lot of the lighthouse in Castleton. The sun hadn't gone down yet, but the light was on already, flashing every few seconds.

There were a few people wandering around, walking their dogs, taking pictures of the sunset and the waves as they crashed against the cliffs where the lighthouse perched.

"I haven't been here before," Ryan said.

"See? There's lots to explore in this little part of the state."

Ryan carried the food down toward the picnic tables.

"You'll have a little more room than you did at Sydney and Lark's table," I said as she swung one leg and then the other over the bench to sit down.

"I wouldn't have gone if I'd known it was going to be that crowded," she said.

"Same," I agreed as I opened my pizza box and pulled two slices onto my paper plate, along with two of the sliders.

Ryan cracked the top of her soda can and I watched her throat as she swallowed. She gazed out over the ocean for a moment.

"You can't beat the view," I said.

"No, you can't," she agreed before selecting a slice of pizza. I waited to take a bite of mine until after she did.

"You're watching me," she said.

"Sorry," I said, flustered at being caught ogling her.

"You can, if you want," she said casually. "I don't mind."

I looked up in surprise and there it was again. That heat pulsing between us like a living thing. I took a shaky breath and forced myself to go back to my pizza.

She took a bite, and then another.

"How is it?" I asked.

"It's not New York or Chicago, but it's respectable," she said.

"We do what we can here in Arrowbridge," I said.

"So," I said, "you don't want to talk about being an heiress, but what can you tell me about yourself? I know practically nothing."

Ryan methodically finished her first slice as she thought.

"What do you want to know?" she asked.

"Literally anything," I said. Everything about her was interesting.

"My favorite color is blue that's almost gray. I have an MBA from UConn that my father made me get. I wanted to study something else. Anything else. My favorite place I've ever visited is Norway. How am I doing?" she said.

"Yeah, no, that's good. I've never been to Norway. I've actually never been out of the US. Not even to Canada. I'd like to go to Europe someday. My favorite color is dark green, and I have a degree in communications from UMass. There. Now we know a little more about each other," I said.

"Do you have a passport?" Ryan asked.

"Yeah, I got one just in case," I said.

"You should travel, if you want," she said.

"It's not that easy. I have work and…life," I said. We were

treading very closely to my anxiety and that was something I absolutely did not want to talk about.

Ryan must have sensed some reluctance because she didn't push it. "Think about it."

"I will," I said. She tried the sliders and said they were good. I'd expected her to have an appetite, but I'd never seen someone demolish an entire pizza and four sliders in one sitting before.

"I feel like I should clap," I said as she wiped her hands on a napkin.

"Stop it," she said, and I swore I could see a blush blooming on her cheeks.

"No, it's a compliment," I said, finishing my soda and sighing. I turned to watch the sunset and it was pretty spectacular.

"It's beautiful, isn't it?" I said.

"Yes," Ryan said in a low voice. A moment later she took the remnants of our meal to the trash and then came back to sit down.

"Do you want to walk around?" I asked.

"Sure," she said. We put my leftovers in the car and made our way around the lighthouse and down toward the rocks. They could be treacherous when wet, but there were a few little paths that you could take that were relatively safe.

I picked my way down, and Ryan followed closely.

"I'm not a klutz, you know," I said.

"You have fallen a few times around me," she said behind me, a hint of a smile in her voice.

"Well that's because—" I started to say, but then stopped myself.

"Because?" she prompted.

"Never mind," I said.

I couldn't tell her that the reason I fell around her was *her*. My legs didn't work properly in her presence. Way too embarrassing to admit.

I took another step and slipped on a loose rock.

"Oh!" I said, but Ryan caught my arm.

"I've got you," she said as I found a better foothold.

"Thanks," I said breathlessly.

"Maybe we should sit down," she said, so we both climbed onto a large boulder that was relatively flat at the top and had room enough for two people to sit side by side.

The air was damp with the salty taste of the ocean. I inhaled the familiar scent and sighed in relief.

"I love that," I said.

"What?" Ryan asked.

"The smell of the ocean. People think it smells like fish, but it doesn't."

She inhaled deeply. "You're right."

The two of us sat there in companionable silence for a while. People being quiet around me sometimes made me anxious, because my mind would go in all kinds of terrible directions and start thinking that they were mad at me, or annoyed, or bored, or giving me silent treatment.

It was different with Ryan, and I didn't know why.

I watched her out of the corner of my eye as the sunset made her hair glow. She really was incredibly beautiful.

I swung my legs back and forth and shivered a little as the temperature dropped.

"Are you cold?" Ryan asked.

"I'm fine," I said.

"Are you? Or are you just saying that?" she asked.

"I'm a little chilly, but it's not a big deal," I said.

She stood up and gave me her hand. "I have an extra jacket in the car. Come on."

My comfort won out and I took her hand as she pulled me to my feet and then helped me navigate my way back up the little path and onto more solid ground.

She dropped my hand and I wished she would have kept holding it.

Ryan pulled a folded fleece out of the backseat and handed it to me.

I started laughing as I put it on, because it nearly reached my knees and could have almost passed as a dress on me.

"Here," Ryan said, helping me roll up the sleeves so I could even find my hands.

"Thank you," I said, trying to be stealthy about smelling the scent that clung to the fleece. It smelled like her.

"You're welcome," she said, reaching down and adjusting the collar of the jacket, her fingers brushing the sides of my neck.

I started trembling, but not because I was cold.

"I should get you home," she said.

"Why?" I asked. It wasn't like I was a teen with a curfew. Sure, I didn't stay out late on the regular, but that was more due to my social anxiety than anything else.

"Is there anywhere else to go in this town?" she asked. "Some hidden bar or nightclub that I'm unaware of?"

"No, but I'm assuming you're renting a house. I wouldn't bring you back to mine unless you want to meet my parents," I said.

Ryan was silent for a second.

"I'm not asking to go back to your house for like, sex. We could just hang out, watch a movie. Talk. Eat the rest of my pizza. Not in a sexual way," I said, the words falling out of my mouth.

Ryan's lips twitched, as if she was hiding a smile.

"So you don't want to come back to my place for sex?" she asked.

"I mean…" I said, fumbling. I had no idea how to answer her question.

"Yes?" she prompted.

Surprised By Her

"Hey, you're the one who kissed me out of the blue," I said. I wasn't trying to throw it in her face, but it had happened.

Ryan nodded. "I did."

"Why?" I asked. "That's been bugging me for weeks. Why did you kiss me?"

Ryan lifted one hand and stroked the side of my face.

"Because I wanted to," she said in a low voice.

"And do you want to do it again?" I asked, not sure if I was ready to hear the answer.

She exhaled through her nose and leaned closer to me. "Yes."

It was difficult to breathe, but I didn't care.

"What's stopping you?" I asked.

"Do you want me to kiss you?" she asked.

Now the spotlight was on me.

"Hell yes," I said, and she chuckled. "Sorry."

"Never apologize for your enthusiasm, Everly," she said. "It's one of your best qualities."

Why were we still talking? Why wasn't she kissing me? As much as I wanted to hear about my other good qualities, I wanted her mouth more, so I took matters into my own hands, reaching up and gripping the back of her neck, pulling slightly to reduce the difference in our heights.

Kissing someone as tall as Ryan required a little bit of maneuvering on both our parts.

Ryan let out a little sound that was so cute that I smiled before our lips met.

After only a tiny bit of contact, Ryan broke the kiss and I found myself being picked up again. This time she set me on the hood of her car and widened her stance.

"There," she said, satisfied, and then she was kissing me again, this time with that same intensity and fierceness from the very first day. I was swept away again, completely lost to physical sensation. Her tongue teased before venturing into my mouth and tangling with mine.

The candle heiress was kissing me, and I'd never experienced anything like this.

Everything was perfect except that the hood of the car wasn't that comfortable. I kept trying to adjust myself, and Ryan noticed.

"Everything okay?" she said in between little kisses.

"Take me to your place," I said. "Please." I wasn't above begging her to take me home. My dignity and pride had gone out the window the moment she kissed me again. Right now I needed her, and I couldn't have her the way I wanted in this parking lot.

She pulled back and I couldn't see her through the lenses of my fogged-up glasses.

"Are you sure?"

"Completely sure," I said, running my hands up her arms. Fuck, I wanted to touch her everywhere. All my social anxiety had left the building. The only thing left inside me was desire.

Ryan lifted me off the car and then opened the passenger door for me. I fell into the seat, still swaddled in Ryan's jacket.

She got into the driver's seat and sped out of the lot, kicking up gravel.

Chapter Eight

"*This is your rental?*" I asked. It was dark, so I couldn't see everything, but there was no mistaking that the house was big. Not as big as Mark's, but still, large. We were down the end of a private road, tucked right into the woods, and this huge house was sitting here.

"I never knew this was here," I said.

"I think they built it two or three years ago," Ryan said, pulling into the garage.

This time I didn't wait for her to open my door, but I did wait for her to open the door that led into the house as the automatic garage door closed.

I followed Ryan through the door and into a bright, open kitchen that was open to a huge living room with high ceilings and wood beams. The space had a modern cabin vibe with a massive brick fireplace, cozy couches, thick rugs, and a neutral palate.

"Wow," I said. "This is gorgeous."

"It works," Ryan said, setting her keys down in a bowl on a side table. "Would you like a drink?"

"Sure," I said, heading from the kitchen toward the living

area. I peered through the window and saw a massive backyard with a patio, a shining grill, a pool, and a gazebo.

"Why do you swim in the ocean?" I asked as she mixed drinks for both of us.

"I don't really like the smell of chlorine," she said as she dropped ice cubes into a glass.

"That makes sense," I said. "The ocean's pretty cold, though."

"I don't mind," she said.

I rejoined her in the kitchen to see what she was making. Ryan carefully moved a peeler across an orange and then added the little strip to the glass and handed it to me.

"What is it?" I asked.

"Negroni," she said. "So you can try it."

"Oh, thank you," I said, taking it from her.

Ryan sipped at her drink, watching me. I took a cautious taste.

"Well?" she asked.

"It's good," I said. "I like it."

"Good," she said before starting to walk out of the kitchen and down a hallway.

"Where are you going?" I asked.

She swiveled around to face me. "My bedroom. Isn't that why you're here?"

I mean, yes, but now that I actually was standing in her house with her with the prospect of having sex with a sexy candle heiress, my anxiety had started to creep its way back into my mind.

"Y-yes, let's go to your bedroom," I said, hating the little stutter in my voice.

Ryan raised an eyebrow but didn't say anything else as she led me down the hall to her room.

"Holy shit," I said when we walked in. The suite was almost as big as the entire downstairs of my parent's house.

Not only was there a huge sitting area with a fireplace, the bed was the biggest one I'd ever seen. French doors probably led to an outdoor deck or something, and then I turned and saw the bathroom.

"Holy shit," I said again. The bathroom was a dream. A big, beautiful tub, a massive shower with multiple showerheads, two sinks, a vanity area, and two separate toilets.

"Hers and hers," I said. "Or his and hers. Or his and his. Or theirs and his. Or—"

Ryan stopped the torrent of words by putting her mouth on mine.

"Come on," she said, taking one of my hands and leading me back into the bedroom.

Ryan sat on the edge of the bed and pulled me between her spread legs.

"Hey, I'm taller than you," I said.

"Not quite," she said, tugging on my shirt to pull me closer.

Our lips met again as my fingers dove into her hair and stroked her arms and pulled at her clothes. She was definitely wearing too many.

"You're so fucking hot," I said.

Ryan chuckled. "Thank you."

"Can I see you?" I asked.

Ryan leaned back and pulled her shirt over her head, revealing a simple black designer bra with the name along the band. I traced her shoulders, reveling in the feel of her musculature. My mouth practically watered at the thought of kissing and tasting her everywhere.

"Your turn, cupcake," she said, and the use of the nickname made me smile.

"Cupcake? Is that what you're calling me now?"

"It suits you," she said, pulling on my shirt again.

I had a moment of self-consciousness as I yanked my shirt over my head and chucked it on the floor.

I hadn't planned on showing her my bra tonight, but I'd worn one of my favorites anyway, made of dark purple lace that complimented my hair. It didn't leave much to the imagination, since my nipples were completely visible through the lace.

"You're beautiful," Ryan said, reaching to the back of my head to pull out the elastic in my hair.

"What's your natural color?" she asked.

I pointed to my roots. "It's like a shade between brown and blonde."

"I like the lavender," she said.

"Me too."

I raked my hands through her hair and kissed her again before reaching back and undoing the clasp of my bra. I tried to slide it of smoothly, but then my arm got caught and Ryan had to help me.

She stared at me for a second before cupping my breasts in her hands, scraping her thumbs across my nipples, causing them to harden.

She brought one to her mouth and kissed my nipple, causing me to jolt with the contact.

Ryan looked up at me through dark lashes as she sucked my nipple into her mouth as she touched the other with her hand.

"Mmmm," I said. "That feels good."

She lifted her head and smiled at me.

"I want you under me," she said.

Imagining Ryan on top of me was absolutely what I wanted as well.

"Yes," I said, and then squealed as she rose to her feet and clasped me to her body at the same time. She turned and laid me gently on the bed.

"I should probably be offended at how easy it is for you to pick me up, but I really like it," I said as she pulled off her joggers and balled them up to be thrown to the other side of the room.

"You played basketball, didn't you?" I said, working my pants down my legs.

Ryan rolled her eyes and crawled onto the bed to lay next to me.

"Yes, I did," she said, her finger tracing down my stomach and stopping just short of my underwear.

"That's hot," I said. "Were you any good?"

"I'll show you pictures of my trophies later," she said. "Right now I want to know what *you* want."

"You. Naked," I said, hooking my finger in the front of her underwear and starting to pull.

"That's a given, cupcake," she said. "Anything specific?"

"This isn't my first time, Ryan," I said.

She smiled and stroked a finger along my side, making me shiver.

"I know, but I think it's best before we go any further to set boundaries and expectations," she said.

"Oh," I said. "That makes sense."

When it came to sex, I'd always just kind of gone with it. Sometimes it had been good, sometimes it had been bad, but I'd never really had a conversation like this with a partner.

"Do you have anything you don't want me to do?" she asked.

"I can't think when you're doing that," I said as she circled my nipple. "I mean... I don't know. I've never really thought about it before."

"How about this: if I do something you don't like, you can just say 'stop.' If you want me to slow down, you can tell me to pause, or that you need a break," she said.

"Sounds fair. Is there anything you don't want?" I asked.

"I can get ticklish sometimes, so if I start laughing, that's probably it. I'm not laughing at you. I'm pretty open about everything, but for now let's just explore and see where it leads us," she said, leaning in and kissing my neck.

"No hickies please," I gasped. I absolutely didn't want to go home and have to explain them to my parents. Sometimes it was like being a teenager again living in my house.

Ryan laughed softly as she straddled me.

"Why are you still wearing these?" I asked, yanking, again, on her underwear.

"We'll take them off at the same time," she said, rolling onto her back. In moments, we were both completely naked and I barely knew what to touch first. I reached for her, but she held up a hand.

"One second," she said, rolling over and giving me a delicious shot of her back and rounded ass as she reached into her bedside table.

"I've got a couple different kinds of lube, and lots of toys and other things if you want," she said.

"You're so accommodating," I said. "That's really hot."

"Is it?" she asked, sliding on top of me. Her arms flexed as she held herself above me.

"You're beautiful, Everly," she said. "Fuck, I love a woman wearing glasses and nothing else."

"Bad eyesight makes Ryan horny, noted," I said, and she laughed.

"I need to kiss you," she said, reaching one hand between my legs and gently stroking my center. "Here."

I gasped and nodded, at a loss for words.

Ryan slunk down my body, leaving little kisses on my skin as she went.

She wasted no time in hooking one of my legs over her shoulder and spreading the other one wide to give her better access.

"So pretty," she said in a reverent voice as she gently

stroked me up and down, fluttering her fingers a little at my entrance, causing me to moan.

Ryan kissed the very top of my core, just above my clit. Since I hadn't been doing any dating lately, or having anyone see me naked, I'd let everything grow out, but Ryan didn't seem to mind.

She kissed my lips, tugging on them slightly before licking me up and down, flicking my clit with her tongue when she reached it.

I ran my hand through her hair, gathering it up so it wasn't in her way. She looked up at me and smiled in a way that almost made me come right then and there.

Ryan nuzzled me at the same time as slipping one, and then two fingers inside me.

I moved my hips toward her, seeking more, and she pushed down on one of my hips.

"Easy, cupcake."

She kissed the inside of my leg that was over her shoulder and then fluttered her fingers inside me with alarming speed.

"Oh, *fuck*," I said.

She gave me another smile before sucking my clit into her mouth so hard that I almost blacked out.

"Beautiful girl," she said, adding another finger and circling my clit with her tongue.

I'd been right about the skill of her fingers, but I hadn't anticipated her tongue. Did she do exercises with that too? The way she flicked it against my clit in just the right spot was nothing short of supernatural.

Those long talented fingers and that dexterous tongue had me almost crying as I begged and moaned and thrashed underneath her.

"Let go, Everly," she said. "Just let yourself go."

Her words were almost a growl and for some reason that was

what it took to detonate an orgasm that clasped my entire body, hitting me from the ends of my hair to my toenails. It went on and on in bursts, and just when I thought it was over, Ryan would wring more out of me as she fucked me with fingers and mouth.

At last, the waves faded and my body slowly came down from whatever dimension I'd just visited. It wasn't earth, that was for sure.

I had never come so fucking hard in my entire life.

My entire body tingled with warmth as I gazed down at Ryan. She set my leg on the bed and kissed me just above my clit, causing me to tremble.

"Good girl," she said. I ran my fingers through her hair, unable to stop staring at her.

"You," I said, still panting a little, "are very talented."

She grinned and dragged herself up to my mouth for a kiss.

AFTER THAT INCREDIBLE PERFORMANCE, I was a bit nervous, and Ryan must have sensed it.

"We don't have to do anything else tonight. That was enough," she said, stroking my hair.

I put a hand on her shoulder and pushed her until she was on her back.

"No, I'm getting you off," I said. "This is happening."

"I'm not complaining," she said, sitting up to kiss me.

As mind-altering as my climax had been, I was vibrating with the need to touch and taste her. My need to explore every single inch warred with my need to fuck her brains out, so I decided on a little bit of both.

I started with her beautiful neck, stroking and kissing and lavishing attention as I ventured down her body.

She had a few freckles on the tops of her shoulders that I

couldn't neglect, so I tasted them before moving on to her breasts, licking and gently biting her nipples to see what she liked. Every single response was precious, and I made note of everything.

I finally got to kiss those precious abs on my way down, and I promised myself that I'd get back to them later. I nuzzled her hips and spread her legs apart, but the angle wasn't right.

"Can you hand me a pillow?" I asked. She pulled one off the top of the bed and passed it to me.

"Hips up, please," I said, and slid it under her, arranging it so I could have better access and then took my glasses off, handing them to her so she could set them on the nightstand.

"All I can think about is you suffocating me with your thighs," I said, stroking one of said thighs. "Not like, really suffocating me, I don't think."

"Breath play is a little more advanced than I'd want to get with you tonight," she said, and I was beginning to realize just how experienced Ryan was, and I had to push it aside or else I was never going to be able to do this.

It didn't matter if she had more experience. I had enthusiasm.

Going with the thigh-crushing idea, I draped both of her legs on my shoulders. She had a whole lot of leg, and I was ecstatic.

She was open to me and already glistening, so I dove right in, tracing my tongue up, around, and down, circling multiple times as her fingers gripped my hair, yanking just a little bit, which sent a bolt of lust through me. Huh.

"Use your fingers," she gasped, her head thrown back as she arched against me.

Doing as she asked, I slid two fingers inside her, feeling the thrill as her inner muscles clamped against them.

"More," she demanded, and I smiled. She might think she was in control, but I was the one who was going to get her off.

I stroked three fingers inside, widening them and then pulling back.

"Do you need more?" I asked as I fucked her with three fingers.

"Yes," she said, her hips bucking against my hand.

"Hand me the lube," I said, and she fumbled on the table to grab one of the bottles, basically throwing it at me. The bottle landed next to her, and I grabbed it. This was uncharted territory for me, but now that I knew it was possible, I couldn't think of anything else.

"Let me know if it's too much," I said.

"Please, Everly," she whined, and I covered my hand with the lube, bringing my fingers together.

"I've got you," I said, slowly pushing my hand inside her. I got about halfway and pulled out, changing the angle.

"Everly," she said, pushing toward me, asking for more, but I wasn't going to rush this. The last thing I wanted was to get carried away and hurt her. Plus, slowly torturing her was more fun.

"I've got you, Ryan. I've got you," I said, stroking her clit as I worked my hand in and out before making it all the way inside. She was so warm and beautiful and she gasped as she pressed a little on my head.

I kissed her clit as I thrust with my hand as her hips pushed against me, fucking herself on my face and my hand.

I felt the orgasm rush forward and take hold of her, making sure to look up so I could see her face when it happened.

Her thighs clasped my head and she pushed herself against my face so I could barely breathe, but it was all completely and totally worth it to see her come apart and lose herself. Her toes curled and dug into my skin, her fingers made marks on my scalp as she rode out the last of her pleasure and then collapsed back on the bed, her entire body relaxing.

I left a little kiss on her clit that made her tremble before I let her legs down and kissed her belly on my way back up her body.

I snuggled in next to her, watching her face.

At last she turned toward me and smiled.

"I'm really glad you spilled coffee on me," she said, pulling me in for a deep kiss.

"YOU'RE WELCOME TO STAY, if you want," she said as we lay together, still naked. We were both sweaty and I needed to pee and wash my hands but moving seemed like too much work.

"I'd like to avoid my parent's interrogation as long as possible," I said.

"Oh, is that the only reason you want to stay?" she asked. Her cheeks were still bright from her climax, and there was a soft playfulness about her that I had only seen glimpses of before.

"Not the *only* reason," I said, sitting up. "I also really want to use your shower."

Ryan laughed and shoved at my shoulder. "Go on then."

I hopped off the bed. "Want to join me?"

Ryan stood up and gave me a quick kiss, as if she couldn't stop herself.

"Of course."

IN ADDITION to the beautiful shower, the bathroom also had robes and a heated towel warmer that I insisted on using.

"Come here," I said to Ryan as I climbed on the stone bench that ran along one wall of the shower. I had a bottle of shampoo in one hand.

She snorted and turned her back so I could soap up her hair. I gave her a little scalp massage as she leaned into me.

She rinsed her head and then did the same for me, working the shampoo through my hair.

"How often do you have to dye your hair?" she asked.

"It fades really fast, so I touch it up myself at home every few weeks. I spend enough money at the salon as it is. Lavender hair is a lifestyle," I said.

"It's lovely," she said.

"Thanks. I'm guessing that's not your natural color," I said, pointing to her hair.

"No, but my real color is only a few shades lighter, so I can get away with not getting it done for a little bit longer."

Things got frisky when we soaped each other's bodies and I couldn't stop myself from reaching between her legs and bringing her to another climax. In retaliation, she made me sit on the bench as she went down on me, the hot water running down my back.

She wrapped me in a robe that was definitely too big for me and I used her comb to detangle my hair.

"I always have a snack before bed," she said as I looked at her bottles and containers of skincare items. They were all super fancy, so I was going to take advantage.

"When are you supposed to start using retinol?" I asked, reading the label on the back.

"When you're older," she said, taking the bottle from me.

"If I start now, it's preventive," I said, reaching for the bottle. She smirked at me as she held it out of reach.

"Remember telling me that you were ticklish?" I said, wiggling my fingers at her.

"Don't you dare," she said, her eyes narrowing.

"Then hand me the retinol," I said, holding my hand out.

She gave it to me, and I smoothed it on my face, enjoying the delicate scent.

"I'm just going to send my parents a message that I'm staying over," I said as she headed toward the kitchen.

She nodded and I shot off a quick message and put my phone on silent to avoid the barrage of questions that my message no doubt set off.

Ryan was searching through the fridge, pulling things out and setting them on the marble countertop.

"Can I help?" I asked.

"Can you grab one of those big plates?" she asked, pointing to a cabinet. I opened it and realized the platters were on the second shelf.

Sighing, I started climbing on the counter.

"What are you doing?" Ryan asked, a block of cheese in one hand.

"Getting the platter," I said, pulling it out and then setting it gently down on the counter.

"Can I get an assist?" I asked, holding my arms out.

Ryan shook her head, but she came over and picked me up off the counter, but she didn't set me down right away.

I ran my fingers through her still-damp hair and kissed her as she held me.

"Thanks," I said in between kisses.

"You're welcome," she said, finally setting me down and grabbing the platter.

I leaned on the counter as she made a snack plate for us with different kinds of cheese and crackers and dried cherries and blood oranges and pistachios.

"Would you like some tea?" she asked.

"Absolutely."

Ryan filled the kettle and this time I was able to reach both the mugs and the selection of tea.

"Here, I got some local honey," she said, handing me a glass bottle. I found the spoons and made up my cup.

"Honey for you?" I asked.

"Please," she said.

Ryan carried the platter and I took charge of the tea as we went back to the bedroom.

"I would eventually like to see the rest of the house, but this is fine for now," I said as we settled in the sitting area of the main bedroom.

Ryan turned on the fireplace and even though it was June, I was all for the cozy vibes.

She set the platter between us and I dragged the second chair closer to hers.

"That's better," I said, reaching for my tea and cradling it in my hands.

"What did your parents say about you staying with me?" she asked.

"I have no idea. I sent the message and put it on silent and that was that. I'll deal with that tomorrow," I said, making a face. At least I didn't have to work. That was a huge relief. Having to drag my ass to the pottery shop and do a full day would have been pretty miserable.

"You could have breakfast with me, prolong the inevitable for a little bit," she said, setting a slice of cheese on a cracker.

"Mmm, depends on what we're having," I said. "If you're only going to microwave a frozen burrito, then I'd have to think about that. If you're making me pancakes from scratch with bacon and fresh fruit, then I'd be more likely to stick around."

"What if I make you a microwaved burrito after I let you sit on my face?" she asked, and I almost slid right out of my chair.

"Oh, well, that would definitely be something to consider," I said, suddenly sweating in the robe.

Ryan laughed softly. "I can make you pancakes, Everly."

I grabbed an orange segment and popped it into my mouth. "Pancakes are my favorite."

RYAN CHANGED the comforter on the bed and gave me a soft T-shirt to wear. I did a little twirl and a curtsy, making her laugh as she brushed her teeth at one of the sinks in the bathroom. She spit in the sink and wiped her face.

"There's an extra toothbrush in the drawer," she said, pointing. The sinks were separated by the vanity and I felt really far away from her, but I pulled the toothbrush out, unwrapping a brand new one and uncapping a fresh tube of toothpaste.

I tried not to read into it that no one else had used it before. It didn't mean she hadn't brought anyone else in Arrowbridge home, but it did make me feel a little happy as I brushed my teeth and joined her back in the bedroom.

"This bed is massive," I said, hopping to get into it.

"It's a little much," Ryan agreed.

"Unless you have multiple partners or a lot of dogs," I said.

"Or both," Ryan said.

"I'd love to have a dog," I said. She was on her back completely on the other side of the bed, so I scooted over until there was less distance between us.

"I had a dog growing up," Ryan said. "His name was Rocket and he had exactly one braincell. My dad hired this celebrity dog trainer to come work with him, but it didn't do any good. He never learned how to sit or stay or anything, but I loved him to bits. My parents had to put him down when I went to college."

She turned her head to look at me.

"He sounds like a good boy," I said.

"He was."

It seemed sex had loosened Ryan's tongue as she told me more about her childhood. It had been very, very different from mine.

"Stop doing that," she said.

"Doing what?" I asked.

"Rolling your eyes when I talk about the country club."

"I'm sorry, I can't help it," I said. "It's just too on the nose."

Ryan sighed. "I went because it was what was expected of me. I did a lot of things that were expected of me."

"When did you come out?" I asked. I'd snuck my hand up to her shoulder and was tracing random patterns on her arm.

"High school. I got caught making out with a girl in the stables at the country club," she said with a smile.

"Ohhh, scandal," I said. "I bet you had all the tongues wagging."

She snorted. "My parents were surprisingly good about it. In fact, the only thing my dad said was that I should have chosen better. A month later her father got indicted for insider trading and her mom moved them all to Texas and I never saw her again."

"Tragic," I said.

"And you?" she asked.

"Well, having two moms, I always knew that being a lesbian was a possibility, but I just never thought it was me. Then I had this really intense toxic friendship with a girl when I was eleven and everything kind of clicked into place. She was straight, of course. I check in on her social media every now and then. She's married to a guy and has two kids. Looks happy."

"Falling for straight girls is the worst," she said, her arm encircling me and pulling me until I was laying on her chest, tucked right in under her chin.

"Agreed," I said through a yawn.

I felt her lips on my head. "Go to sleep, cupcake."

THERE WERE a lot of things I didn't know about Ryan, but I found out the next day that she was a morning person.

Way too early I felt her move and get out of bed.

"I'm going for a run," she said in my ear.

"Okay," I mumbled, still not awake.

"I'll be back in a while and I'll make you pancakes."

"Mmmm," I said.

"Go back to sleep," she said.

THE NEXT TIME I woke up, I heard the shower. It was still too early for me, but I sat up and looked around. Was the room bigger now than it had been last night? It felt bigger.

Ryan came out of the bathroom in just a towel and I couldn't stop staring.

"Good morning," she said.

"Good morning," I said through a yawn. "You were up early."

"I usually am," she said. "I'm starving, are you ready for breakfast?"

"Sure," I said, even though my stomach wasn't awake yet. I got out of the huge bed and went to pee as Ryan got dressed. Since I only had my outfit from last night, I just kept her T-shirt on and wandered out to the kitchen to find Ryan pulling ingredients from the cabinets. She'd put on a tank and a pair of loose shorts.

"Need help?" I asked, raising my arms above my head in a stretch. Ryan stared at me and didn't answer. I looked down and saw that my nipples were completely visible through the shirt.

"Ryan?" I asked.

"Huh?" she said, her gaze moving up to my face.

"I asked if you needed help with breakfast?" I said, fighting a smile.

She blinked and nodded. "Can you pull out the bacon?"

I got the bacon from the fridge as Ryan started mixing batter for pancakes from a recipe on her phone.

"You wouldn't happen to have any chocolate chips on hand, would you?" I asked.

"I might," she said, opening a cupboard and pulling out a bag.

"Amazing. You have everything," I said.

"I wouldn't go that far. I'll let you decide how many you want," she said, passing me the bag.

"You're giving me so much power," I said, holding the bag in two hands.

"Don't let it go to your head," she told me, mixing the batter. I ripped the bag open and started dumping the chips in.

"These pancakes are going to be half chocolate," Ryan said as she stirred them in.

"Exactly," I said. "Why is it that breakfast is the only meal where you can essentially eat a dessert and it's considered fine and balanced?"

"I have no idea," Ryan said, taking the bowl to the stove. I dealt with the bacon, laying it out in a pan and turning the oven on to preheat.

"My parents always made it in the oven instead of on the stove," I said.

"Less splatter that way," Ryan said. "Do you want eggs?"

"I can make scrambled and that's about it," I said. "Every single time I've tried to fry an egg, I've busted the yolk. I think I'm egg cursed."

Ryan snorted. "Scrambled is fine." She poured dollops of batter onto a long griddle pan as I cracked eggs into a bowl and added a splash of cream and salt and pepper before I whipped them together.

Cooking with Ryan in this elaborate kitchen felt far more domestic than it should. We still barely knew each other, but this felt like something girlfriends would do together on the weekend.

"Can we eat in the gazebo?" I asked when everything was ready.

"If you want to," she said.

We carried everything outside and I let out a happy sigh as we sat down together. The backyard was absolutely beautiful and included a small garden, several bird feeders, and a little path that led under a trellis into the woods.

"I can't picture you gardening," I said.

"I don't, really," she said. "Someone else does and the owner pays them very well to maintain everything."

I stacked pancakes on my plate and added butter and syrup. Ryan filled her plate with bacon and eggs and only one pancake.

"You're missing out," I said, cutting a bite and shoving it into my mouth, syrup dripping down my chin.

Ryan reached out and used her thumb to swipe up the syrup.

"I'm not much of a sweet breakfast person," she said.

"I guess that means more for me," I said, taking another bite. "These are really good."

I should probably worry about looking like a mess in front of her, but I was hungry and the food was really good and I'd literally had my hand inside her last night so I didn't think having some chocolate on my face was going to matter.

"What are your plans for the rest of the day?" I asked.

"Can't get enough of me, can you?" she said, arching an eyebrow as she ate another slice of bacon.

"No, I was just wondering what you're doing." I didn't want to seem like a clinger.

"The plan was to head to the beach for a swim and come

back here for lunch, maybe go for a drive, get a little lost, come back here and read for a bit, have dinner and soak in the bath." All of that sounded amazing and wasn't that far off what I would have done in her situation.

"Sounds like a great Saturday," I said. "I was just going to sit outside and read and maybe clean out my closet, but I like your day better."

Ryan ate her last piece of bacon carefully.

"What are your feelings about putting off the closet cleaning?" she asked, looking up from her plate.

"I don't know, it's a huge mess. I have to go through all my clothes," I said, sitting back in my chair. "What are you offering as an alternative?"

"You and me, naked. More food, definitely. A walk on the beach. A drive anywhere within an hour of Arrowbridge, which isn't saying much. More sex." She leaned toward me, using one finger to draw my face closer to hers.

"Maybe just the sex," she said, kissing me. Within seconds, I was cradled in her lap as she kissed me hard, tasting of chocolate and syrup and warm butter and coffee.

"Okay, but I definitely need food again at some point," I said, breaking the kiss.

Ryan smiled. "Don't worry. I'll feed you."

THIS TIME I rode Ryan's hand outside as the birds twittered and I let myself be as loud as I wanted since no one could hear me.

Her fingers slipped from my body and I winced but then gasped when she slid them into her mouth.

"Better than pancakes," she said.

"Your turn," I said, stroking my hand down her stomach.

"Let's go inside," she said, cradling my ass and squeezing it.

"We can leave the crumbs for the birds and get the dishes later."

I hopped off her lap and she stood up.

"Hey, can you bend down," I said, and she gave me a puzzled look.

"Come on, lean down," I said.

She did and I went around to her back and put my arms around her neck.

"Ready?" I asked and she seemed to know what I was trying to do.

"Go," she said, and I jumped as she grabbed my legs in the piggyback position, hoisting me up higher.

"Oh, this is fun," I said, leaning forward to speak in her ear. "Now I get to see the world from your position."

She laughed and carried me into the house, fumbling a little with the sliding door. She didn't let me down until she dumped me on the bed in her bedroom.

I bounced on the mattress and laughed.

"That was fun," I said. "Thanks for the ride."

Ryan gazed down at me with a speculative look on her face.

"What is it?" I asked.

"How do you feel about toys?" she asked.

I sat up and grinned at her. "Big fan. What did you have in mind?"

Ryan looked excited as she pulled something from under the bed. It looked like a vintage trunk, but it was probably new and distressed on purpose.

"Is that your goodie box?" I asked, turning onto my stomach and scooting to the end of the bed to watch her open it.

"I didn't bring my entire collection, just my favorites. I didn't plan on being with anyone this summer," she said, unlocking the trunk and opening the lid.

Each toy had its own little cushioned spot. I'd never seen anything like it, and I'd seen Ezra's collection on display.

"You'd get along with Joy's girlfriend, Ezra. She does sex toy reviews," I said.

"I'd like to talk to her," she said, looking up at me, her eyes bright.

The box had trays on the top and I assumed there was more underneath, but for now, she selected a sleek black vibrator and then shut the trunk.

"Is it charged? I can't count how many times I've been just about to come and the damn thing died."

"You should see what happens when I regularly charge everything," Ryan said. "It's chaos."

"I bet," I said. "Hand it over."

She gave me the vibrator and I turned it on. A soft buzzing filled the room.

"Nice," I said and looked up at her. "Get naked."

Ryan pulled everything off and I did the same. It would have felt strange to be clothed when she wasn't.

Ryan lounged back on the pillows, a satisfied look on her face.

"You look like a queen," I said, crawling up toward her to give her a kiss. I turned the vibrator on the lowest setting and skated it across her nipples, making her jump and twitch.

I skipped her stomach so it didn't tickle and ran the vibrator up and down her center, coating it in her wetness.

I teased her clit with whisper soft touches before turning the level up, making Ryan let out a gasp.

"Inside, I need it inside," she said, so I dipped the vibrator inside her before quickly removing it and circling her clit with it and repeating the sequence.

Ryan gasped and arched. "V-vibrator inside, need your mouth on my clit." She was already incoherent, which was very satisfying for me.

"Whatever the queen demands," I said, scooting down her body. She handed me the pillow I'd used last night and lifted her hips for me.

I snuggled down into my favorite spot and worked the vibrator all over her until I slid it all the way inside, searching for the right angle she needed. I absorbed every one of her movements and sounds and found the right place that made her beg. I moved the vibrator in and out and once I had that down, I added my mouth, slicking it up and down her clit and then giving that fluttering thing a shot and she really liked that.

"Harder," she begged, so I turned up the vibrator and thrust it harder as I used my mouth until her hips clamped around my head and her entire body convulsed with her climax.

Once her body was calm, I pulled out the vibrator and turned it off.

Ryan was glowing and I just had to kiss her. She gripped the back of my neck and kissed me back fiercely.

"That was really good," she said, pressing her forehead against mine.

"I like playing with your toys," I said. "I think yours are nicer than mine."

"I don't let anything second rate near this," she said, pointing below the waist.

"Does that include me?" I asked.

"You," she said, tapping my nose, "are first rate."

Chapter Nine

"So, I know you aren't a huge fan of pools, but do you mind if I use it?" I asked, sitting up in bed. I wanted to take advantage of this situation while I could.

"Go ahead," Ryan said.

I stood up and pretended to remember something. "Oh no, I don't have anything to swim in. I guess I can't."

Ryan laughed. "I think I can get over my pool aversion if you're going to be skinny dipping."

"That's the spirit!" I said as we went to rinse off in the shower first.

The pool wasn't very warm, but at least it was warmer than the ocean. I slid into the shallow end and paddled around as Ryan dove into the deep end and then swam toward me.

"I was on the swim team in high school," she said when she reached me.

"Then why do you hate pools?" I asked.

"Because I've spent too much time in them," she said, making a face.

"That makes sense," I said. "Were you any good?"

She didn't answer for a second. "I did all right."

Her face told me otherwise.

"You were really good, weren't you?" I asked.

She smirked. "I did all right."

"You don't have to be modest. I bet you got all the trophies and medals," I said. "I bet your parents bragged about you all the time."

Ryan's face fell a little bit. "My parents aren't like your parents."

"What does that mean?" I asked, genuinely curious.

She dove under the water and came up again, shaking water out of her hair.

"What happened when you got good grades in school? What did your parents do?" she asked. I guess we were back to talking about me.

"They'd get me a gift card to my favorite store and take me out for pizza," I said.

"Exactly. No matter what my grade was, my parents would ask why it wasn't higher. Why I wasn't the best student in my class," she said. "I tried to be. I did the sports and studied for the tests and went to the goddamn country club and did all the things I was supposed to do, and it was never enough," she said, breathing heavy. "It was never enough."

I swam close to her and touched her face as I stood up. "I'm sorry."

She stood up and looked down at me. "It's not your fault."

"I know. I'm still sorry though. You deserved to be celebrated for your accomplishments."

Mama still had a bunch of my awards and other things displayed in a case in her office. Anytime my name appeared in the local paper, she'd cut out the article and save it. Those were also framed and up around the house. When I'd been a kid, I'd thought every parent was like that.

"It doesn't matter," she said, swimming away and leaning on the edge of the pool, her feet drifting in the water.

I went over to join her. "It does, but we can talk about something else if we need to," I said.

"I'd rather talk about *anything* else," she said.

I pushed back from the wall and smiled at her. "How long can you hold your breath?"

Ryan grinned, seeing the challenge in my eyes. "Longer than you."

"Wanna bet?" I asked.

"You're on," she said.

"IT'S NOT FAIR. Your lungs are bigger," I said when I lost the fifth breath-holding contest by a lot.

"Your body has other benefits," she said.

"Oh, like what?" I asked and then she picked me up. I wrapped my legs around her waist and tried not to grind myself on her abs.

"You're the perfect size, for one," she said, slowly spinning around.

"And?" I asked.

"Your tits are also the perfect size."

"And?" I asked.

"How about we rinse off in the shower and I can show you?" she said.

"Deal."

AFTER ANOTHER SHOWER, I put on some of Ryan's clothes and we headed to the kitchen for snacks that we ended up eating on the couch together. Ryan's legs kept twitching.

"You okay over there?" I asked.

"I'm not good at relaxing," she said. "You know how I told you about my plans for the day? I lied."

I grabbed another handful of popcorn. "Uh huh."

"I lied," she said, putting both hands on her legs. "I was going to run and swim and then do some weights and then mow the yard and then go for a walk with an audiobook and then clean out the fridge. I spend a lot of weekends at Uncle Mark's, but the family is on a camping trip this weekend," she said.

"That sounds like a lot," I said.

"I know," she said, and I swore her cheeks were a little red. "I just… I'm not good at this."

"At sitting?" I asked.

"Yes, sitting and doing nothing." She turned toward me, and I saw a kind of frantic gleam in her eyes.

"We're not doing nothing. We're snacking. And I'm relaxing. I work all week so my weekends are super important," I said.

"I came here to figure out what the fuck I'm doing with my life and to try and relax for the summer, but it turns out I have no idea what I'm doing," she said. "What kind of person doesn't know how to relax?"

"What were you doing before you came here?" I asked.

"I worked for my father," she said, clenching her hands again. "And then I quit."

"Why did you quit?" I asked.

Ryan flexed her fingers and let out a tense breath.

"It's complicated," she said, her jaw tight. I waited for her to say more, but she didn't. "A lot of shit happened to me earlier this year."

"Are you going to get another job?" I asked.

"I don't know," she said. "I still have my trust fund, and a percentage of the company, so I'm not destitute. Not that I need daddy's money," she said, her tone turning defensive.

I put my hands up. "Hey, I didn't say anything. If my parents were rich, they would have had a trust fund for me." As it was, they'd busted their asses to help me pay for college, so I'd graduated with debt, but not as much as some of my classmates. I was grateful for every single cent they'd given me.

"I sound like a spoiled little rich girl," she muttered under her breath.

I reached out to take her hands. "Hey. We don't have to talk about this either. Let's focus on the relaxing part. I really like the idea of taking a walk, but something tells me your idea of a walk and mine are two different things. So." I stood up and held out my hand. "Come take a walk with me."

"YOU HAVE to stop walking so damn fast," I said as I struggled to keep up with the amazon pacing in front of me.

"Sorry," she said, slowing down.

"We're strolling. And I have short legs," I said, taking even smaller steps.

"Fair enough," she said with a laugh.

I'd wanted to head into the woods behind the house, but I'd only had a pair of sandals from the night before, and I didn't want to risk it, so we were walking on the driveway that led down to the house.

"Take a big deep breath," I said, and she gave me a skeptical look, but followed my lead and breathed.

"See? We're relaxing," I said. "We don't need to be anywhere, or go anywhere, or do anything. Listen to the birds."

Ryan looked up and around.

"What kind of birds are those?" she asked.

"I have no idea," I said. "But that's not the point."

"What is the point?" she asked.

"To notice the birds. To notice the smells around you and the feel of the ground underneath your feet."

"It's pavement," she said.

I stopped walking. "Oh my god, you are going to make this difficult, aren't you? Just go with it, Ryan."

"Okay, cupcake," she said.

I walked over to the side of the road and picked two dandelions.

"Rub it under your chin," I said, doing the same. Ryan stared at me in confusion.

"Just do it," I said.

She did and I got up on my tiptoes to inspect it.

"Yup, it's true. How's mine?" I asked, tipping my head up.

"What am I looking for?" she asked.

"Is my chin yellow?" I asked.

"Yes?"

"Good."

I started walking again.

"What does yellow chin mean?" she asked.

I grabbed some more flowers. Daisies and black-eyed Susans and some other flowers I didn't know the names of.

"You want to know what it means?" I asked, presenting Ryan with the bouquet.

"Yes," she said, taking the flowers from me.

I leaned close to her and kissed her softly.

"It means you like butter," I said.

"What?" she asked.

"It means you like butter," I said. "Do you like butter?"

She kissed me back. "I do."

"WHAT NOW?" Ryan asked when we got back to the house.

"Oh, am I in charge of this now?" I asked as she filled a

vase with water and put the wildflowers in it, setting them in the center of the kitchen island.

"You have better ideas than I do," she said, bracing her forearms on the countertop.

"Okay. Are you hungry?" I asked. The snack hadn't been that long ago, but it was lunchtime.

"I'm always hungry, Everly. Literally always."

"Okay. Lunch. Lunch, and we're going to find something really pointless on TV and watch it while we eat."

Ryan nodded. "Okay."

"ARE YOU STILL AVOIDING YOUR PHONE?" Ryan asked as we lounged together on the couch.

"Yup. I'm sure it's traumatized by how many messages my parents have sent wondering when the hell I'm coming home." I made a face. "I should probably check it just to make sure there isn't any kind of emergency."

I made a face and went to get my phone from the bedroom.

As I suspected, there were a flurry of messages from my parents that I ended up ignoring, a funny meme from Sydney, and that was about it. The lack of messages from people other than my parents might have made me a little depressed under normal circumstances, but right now, I was hanging out with Ryan Jewel. Nothing could bother me right now.

"No emergencies?" Ryan asked when I returned. She'd paused the TV show. As if I'd even been paying attention to it.

I flopped down next to her and leaned on her shoulder. It was very comfortable.

"No emergencies," I said, and she started the show again.

"So, this is relaxing," she said a few moments later.

"Yup. This is relaxing."

She leaned back and put her arm around me, pulling me closer. I pulled my feet up onto the couch and snuggled into her chest.

I felt her kiss my head.

"I think I like relaxing."

AS MUCH AS I didn't want to, I really needed my own clothes and to go home and see my parents. Usually after being with another non-family person for this long, I would have been absolutely fried and would have hit my limit the night after only a few hours.

Things were different with Ryan. She didn't demand anything of me. If I didn't want to talk, she didn't care. There was something about her presence that felt like sinking into a warm, scented bath after a long day. The strain I usually felt with others was just gone. I'd never experienced anything like it with someone I'd just met.

"I don't know how I'm going to relax without you," Ryan said as she drove me home after I'd put my other outfit back on.

"You'll figure it out. I can message you ideas," I said.

She pulled in front of my house far too soon and I leaned over to her.

"I really want to kiss you right now, but I know my parents are watching out the window," I whispered.

"Why are you whispering?" she whispered.

"Because I feel like they can still hear me," I whispered.

She laughed and then pulled me close.

"I'm going to kiss you anyway," she told me just before her lips met mine.

All too soon she pulled away and I was left breathless again.

"Okay, that was worth it," I said.

"Good," she said, and it was time to go. "I'll send you updates on my relaxing."

"Please do," I said, getting out of the car and heading into the house without looking back.

~

MY PARENTS WERE on me the second I closed the door.

I put both hands up.

"Can you just hit the pause button for a second until I change my clothes?" I asked as Mama bounced on her toes and made little noises as if the words she wanted to say were struggling to get out of her mouth.

"Yes," Mom said, gripping Mama's arm. "We'll just be down here when you're ready."

I walked up the stairs and closed the door of my room with a happy sigh before going to my dresser and pulling out a new outfit.

Not a bad weekend at all.

~

"IS THIS SOMETHING SERIOUS WITH RYAN?" Mama asked as she cooked dinner.

"For the hundredth time, I don't know," I said. "Probably not. She's like, an heiress, she's older, and she needs to get her life together, so I'm the last thing she needs."

My phone buzzed with a new message, and it was from Ryan.

How am I doing? She sent with a picture of herself sitting on the grass outside the house.

My god, she was so fucking hot.

Very good I responded.

"Sweetie?" Mama said, drawing my attention back.

"Huh?" I asked.

"Are you talking to your girlfriend?" she asked, so much hope in her eyes.

"She's *not* my girlfriend," I said for the hundredth time. I shared a look with Mom, who shrugged.

"But she could be," Mama sang, doing a little twirl in the kitchen.

I should probably try to get through to her, but it felt like a losing battle. If Mama wanted to think of Ryan as my girlfriend, whatever. She was leaving in a few months anyway and that would be the end of that. I guess I'd have to make the most of the time I had with her.

I know I left you a few hours ago, but I think I might need some help relaxing tomorrow. Can you help me? She sent.

I couldn't help but smile as I typed my response. **I think I can help you** I responded.

"Is that her?" Mama said, right next to my ear. I jumped, not realizing that she'd snuck over to me.

"Don't do that. You almost gave me a heart attack," I said, putting my hand on my chest.

"I looked her up online, you know. She looks tall," Mama said.

"She is," I said. "Very tall."

RYAN RANDOMLY SENT me messages for the rest of the evening and told me the next day that she'd pick me up at ten a.m. for our relaxing. This time I made sure my underwear set was cute and I'd meticulously shaved my legs and done a body scrub to make sure my skin was soft and smooth. Ryan had already seen me naked, obviously, but I hadn't been able to make a really good impression on her, so now I wanted to make up for it. I even busted out my fancy hair tool that my parents had gotten me for Christmas a few years ago and curled my hair after I touched up my color. My roots were starting to come in and I needed to make an appointment to get them done again. Still, it was more effort than I'd put into my look in a while.

I even washed my glasses and swapped out a few of my earring hoops for new ones.

All in all, I was the most prepared I'd ever been for relaxing with an incredibly hot and tall woman.

"I made lemon rosemary hummus. And beer cheese," Mama said as I came downstairs to wait for Ryan. She'd been early last time, so I'd made sure to leave enough time to be ready so I wasn't running downstairs with my hair half done when she got here.

Mama held out the insulated carrying bag, one of many that she owned, with a hopeful look on her face.

"Mama, you don't have to keep doing this stuff," I said, but I took the bag from her.

"I know. I wanted to. Please tell her she's welcome to come over for dinner or lunch or any meal, really. We'd love to meet her," Mom said.

"I will," I said, hearing someone pulling into the driveway. I peered out the curtain and saw her car.

"Bye, love you!" I called, yanking the door open, but Ryan was already coming toward me.

"Hi, let's go," I said, giving her a meaningful look.

"We will. Right after I say hello to your parents," she said, as if this was a completely normal thing.

I held my hand up to stop her from coming closer. "You want to meet my parents?"

She nodded once. "Yes."

I opened my mouth to argue and then slammed it shut.

"Okay. Don't say I didn't warn you. Mama made hummus and beer cheese." I held up the bag.

"I'll have to thank her," Ryan said with a tight smile.

Before I could say anything else, the door banged open.

"Sorry," Mom said, not looking very sorry.

"Mom, this is Ryan Jewel. Ryan, this is my mom Lee," I said, pointing to Mom, who shook Ryan's hand.

"I'm Everly's Mama, Lydia," Mama said, almost jumping up and down as she reached for Ryan's hand. "Can I give you a hug?" At least she'd asked.

"Uh, sure," Ryan said as Mama threw herself at Ryan with way too much enthusiasm. Mama grabbed on and Ryan gave me a startled look.

"It's so nice to meet you, Ryan," Mama said, her eyes a little shiny.

This was too much.

"Okay then, we should go," I said, speaking loudly.

"So nice to meet you," Ryan said.

"It was wonderful to meet you," Mama said, reaching for Mom's hand.

I waved to them as we walked to the car. Ryan held my door for me.

"Are they watching?" she asked in my ear.

I glanced toward the door as I got in the passenger seat, the bag of dip on my lap.

"Oh yeah," I said, glaring at my parents and then giving them a wave.

Ryan laughed softly before walking around and getting in. She turned on the car and gave my parents a wave before backing out.

"They're lovely, your parents," she said after a thoughtful silence.

"They're a bit much," I said. "I hope you like beer cheese."

"I have never eaten beer cheese in my life, and I have no

idea what beer cheese even is, but I'm interested to find out," she said, laughing.

"It's good. You'll like it. No one does a dip like Mama," I said.

"Looking forward to it."

"WELL? WHAT DO YOU THINK?" I asked. We were on Ryan's couch with multiple bowls of the chips and crackers Ryan had on hand.

Ryan had just scooped up a serving of beer cheese and tossed it right into her mouth. She chewed thoughtfully.

"I love it," she said, reaching for another chip and taking a bigger serving.

"I'm so happy I can widen your horizons into the field of beer cheese," I said.

"I feel like we should be watching football right now," she said. "Beer cheese seems like a football food."

I dunked a bagel chip into the bowl of hummus. "Do you like football?"

Ryan shrugged. "My dad has a stake in a team, but I've never really enjoyed it."

"Your dad owns a football team?" I asked.

"He owns *part* of a football team. A very, very small part," she said, holding her pointer finger and thumb a millimeter apart.

I thought about asking further questions, but did I really want to know? Not really.

"Are you a football fan?" she asked me after a tense silence.

"I watch with Mom, but it's not my sport," I said.

"What is your sport?"

I shrugged. "Anything where women are being really hot I'm a fan of."

That made her laugh. "I like the way you think."

"Thank you."

"HAVE you started the book club book yet?" I asked.

"No, I haven't. You?"

I shook my head and pushed the last of the beer cheese bowl toward her.

Ryan looked thoughtful for a moment and then got up. She came back a little bit later with the book in her hands.

"Want to read it together?" she asked. I scraped the rest of the hummus out of the bowl and set it down.

"That sounds like a very relaxing thing to do. You're really getting the hang of this," I said.

Ryan smiled easily and my heart did a little fluttering thing that was extremely distracting. Why was she so damn attractive? It was hard to take.

"I'm not a professional voice actor or anything, so don't judge me too harshly," she said before opening the cover and turning to the first page of the book. Ryan started to read in a smooth voice, and I lay back on the couch to watch her as she spoke.

Not a bad way to relax at all.

RYAN PAUSED a while later and coughed. "I'm not used to reading aloud this much."

"I'll get you some water," I said, standing up and touching her shoulder.

"Oh, thanks," she said.

I brought back ice water for both of us and Ryan nearly drained the whole glass before starting again. She was right, she didn't do funny voices or a dramatic reading, but her reading was soothing and straightforward and I liked it. I really liked it.

The story was soft and sweet and precious and totally lived up to the hype so far.

Eventually her voice got tired and she put the bookmark the bookstore had given her between the pages and set it on the coffee table.

"I can't remember the last time someone read to me. I mean, other than an audiobook," I said.

"Did your parents read to you?" she asked.

"Every night for years," I said.

"That's nice," she said. There was no point in asking if her parents had read to her.

"Did you have a nanny growing up?" I asked.

"Several," she said.

"Hold on, several nannies?" I asked. "Why would you need several nannies?"

She gave me a smile which was just her lips pressed together. "Ask my parents."

"Pass," I said. "It doesn't matter. I'm not, like, judging you for the way you grew up. I mean, I might tease you a little bit, but you can tease me right back. There's lots of things you can tease me about. Ryan, I am twenty-six years old and I live with my parents. That's so much material right there. Mama sneaks into my room and cleans it. She will literally wait until I'm not home and steal my hamper to do my laundry because I don't believe in separating whites and colors. My point is, I'm not trying to be an asshole about your past."

Ryan studied me for a few moments. "Thank you," she said.

"No problem," I told her.

"YOU KNOW," she said later as we were making dinner in the outdoor kitchen, "we could relax and go out. I know there's not a lot of places nearby, but there are a few."

"I'm up for going somewhere," I said. "Maybe next weekend?"

"Or," she said, slicing a tomato, "you could have dinner with me earlier than that." She looked up and met my eyes.

"You want to have dinner with me next week?" I tried not to sound too eager.

"Yes," she said, going back to the tomato. She'd said she had barely used the grill, so now was as good a time as any. I had to slap at a few mosquitoes, but Ryan had found a bunch of citronella candles and had the fire pit going.

"I'd like that," I said. "I'd really like that."

"Good. Are you okay if I surprise you?"

I nodded. "Yeah, that's the good kind of surprise. Throwing me a party and inviting a bunch of people to scream at me is not a good surprise."

She nodded and went to check the burgers. "I'll make a note of that. No surprise parties for Everly."

"Thank you," I said, stealing a slice of tomato.

Ryan flipped the burgers and checked the corn and veggie kebabs.

"We are almost ready here," she said, handing me a plate.

"I have anxiety," I blurted out. "Like, actual diagnosed social anxiety. I don't normally tell people, but, uh, I thought you should know. Since we're going to be hanging out."

Ryan didn't let go of the plate, so we just stood there, both holding onto it.

"I knew. Sort of. Not specifically, but I could tell you were stressed out at Layne's party. Is it being in groups of people that does it?"

I added a bun to my plate, and she set the burger on it.

"Parties, yeah. Restaurants. Anywhere that's unfamiliar,

where I don't know what the expectations are. It's like...you know that feeling when you have to get up and speak to a big group of people? I feel like everyone gets stage fright, but the difference is that my body tells my mind that stage fright is on the same level as someone trying to kill me." I'd thought a lot about how to explain my anxiety to someone else and that was the best that I'd come up with. Everyone, on some level, felt anxiety from time to time. The difference was the frequency, the symptoms, and the severity.

Ryan nodded and began to fill her own plate.

I built up my burger and then grabbed a drink from the outdoor fridge.

"Do you ever have panic attacks?" she asked.

"Oh yeah," I said. "I have medication, but I have to take it at the right time and sometimes they creep up on me. I have a therapist I work with too that helps me." I hadn't planned on telling her that part, but I guess I was going all out now.

"Therapy," Ryan said, slicing her burger in half. "I should probably look into that someday."

"I'm not going to say that all therapy is good, or that everyone needs it, but I've had really good luck with mine and she's helped me a lot," I said.

Ryan kept talking, asking me more questions about therapy, about when my anxiety had started, and it was all...comfortable. Easy. I didn't feel any kind of judgment or weirdness. Talking to Ryan was a revelation.

After dinner she took me inside and fucked me slowly in her bed, making me come twice before she would even let me touch her. We showered off and I got dressed in the change of clothes I'd shoved into my bag. The plan was to tell my parents I went in the pool, which would explain why I was coming home with wet hair and a different outfit. They would know it was a lie, and I would know it was a lie, but we would pretend and I wouldn't have to answer any weird questions about my sex life.

"I don't want to go to work tomorrow," I said, petting her abs. I couldn't keep my hands off them in moments like these. We were both drowsy and cuddly in the aftermath of the shower.

"I don't know what I'm going to do with myself," she said.

"What did you do before you met me?" I asked.

Ryan combed through my hair with her fingers. "I was really bored most of the time. I did a lot of just driving around in circles and working out until I fell asleep. And eating."

"That's really sad, Ryan," I said. "You need to find some other hobbies. I can help you think of some, if you want."

"Reading is a good hobby," Ryan said.

"It is. But you're the kind of person who needs like six hobbies. You're a doer, Ryan. You like to do things. It's obvious. We just need to find you new things to do," I said, tracing my finger down her nose.

"Sex is another hobby," she said, stroking my core.

"Mmmm, a very good one," I said, arching into her.

Chapter Ten

Monday morning was a rude awakening. Extremely rude. I'd been floating in a post-orgasmic haze after leaving Ryan's, and my alarm completely cut right through it and blasted me back to reality.

Rude.

"Whoa, you had a good weekend," Sydney said when I walked in the door of the pottery shop. Normally I was thrilled to get to work every day, but today I would so much rather be in Ryan's bed. Naked. Having sex and thinking about hobbies.

"What do you mean?" I asked, touching my hair. I'd showered last night when I got home from Ryan's so there was no way I had sex hair still, but I was a little paranoid anyway.

"You just look all satisfied and relaxed. Did you go get a massage or something?" she asked.

"Yeah, something like that," I said, nodding and making myself as busy as I could so she wouldn't ask me any further questions.

"If I was just your friend and not your boss and your friend, I'd say it looks like you got your back blown out. But since I'm your boss, I'm not going to say that," she said, giving me a significant look.

I just stared at her. Sydney had a tradition of saying what some might consider inappropriate things, but it didn't bother me. Or at least, it hadn't bothered me until just now.

"I don't know what you're talking about," I mumbled, feeling my entire face completely flame up.

"Uh huh," she said, smirking and bumping her shoulder against mine.

"Shut up," I said under my breath, causing her to laugh.

"I'm going to pack boxes," I said, my voice too loud.

"You do that," Sydney said, still cackling.

THE REST of my day dragged in a way that it hadn't ever before. I still had a good time and packed my boxes and helped customers and did all the normal things, but all of my usual tasks paled in comparison to my messages from Ryan.

She sent them consistently throughout the day and I treasured each one of them. There were pictures and jokes and I got a good taste of her dry humor.

You're funny, you know that? I sent her.

Thanks. So are you, cupcake she responded.

Before I'd started hanging out with her, I would have thought we'd have nothing in common, nothing to actually talk about. Our lives had been as different as night and day. Every now and then she'd say something that would remind me just how different. Those little realizations nagged at me, but I just kept telling myself that those things didn't matter because it wasn't like she was my girlfriend. We weren't dating. We weren't building a life together. There was no situation in which I would be part of her world. She was just hanging out in mine for a little while. Everything with Ryan was temporary, which made it more precious. More valued. That was better than not ever knowing her at all. Wasn't it?

～

I KNOW we said we'd make plans sometime this week, but what are you doing tonight? Ryan asked a few minutes before close. I couldn't help the goofy grin from spreading on my face.

My parents will be sad I'm missing dinner, but they'll be thrilled at the reason for it I responded.

We can bring them back some dessert she sent.

There was a sweetness to Ryan that I hadn't expected but was a pleasant surprise. I knew the whole "living with my parents" thing might be a red flag or a dealbreaker for some people, but she hadn't said or done anything that led me to believe she judged me for it. She'd been an amazing listener when I'd spoken about my anxiety and had asked thoughtful questions. Everything about her was just…

They'll love that I replied.

～

"I HAVE NOTHING TO WEAR!" I yelled as I tore through my closet. Ryan was picking me up in twenty minutes and I had nothing to wear. Nothing to wear to a nice restaurant anyway. None of my clothes were appropriate.

"Sweetie, what is it? You're making a lot of noise," Mama said, leaning against the doorway of my closet and looking at the mess I'd made on the floor.

"I don't know what to wear," I said, sitting down in the heap. This was going to be a pain in the ass to clean up, but I was going to deal with that later. Right now I still had to find something to wear.

"What about your Christmas dress?" she asked.

I gave her a face. "Mama, that's obviously a velvet winter dress. I'm going to look silly wearing a very obvious winter dress out in June," I said.

Mama started going through the things I'd already discarded and holding them up.

"What about this?"

"No, it's not right," I said, discarding one choice after another.

Once we'd been through all the options again, she held up one finger and then left the room.

"Okay, I guess I'm on my own now," I said to the empty closet and all my clothes.

Mama came back with a long light-green dress with straps.

"This was mine. I've been saving it to see if I can get back into it. It's vintage, so it's in," she said, handing me the dress.

"This is never going to fit me," I said, but Mama just pointed toward the bathroom.

I went in and slid off my clothes and pulled the dress on. The zipper was in the side seam so I could do it myself.

Somehow, by a miracle or sorcery or something else, the dress did fit. Not only did it fit, but it was the right length for me. It didn't drag on the ground or look completely disproportionate on my body.

"Holy shit," I said, turning to look at myself in the mirror at all angles.

"Well?" Mama said, gently knocking on the door.

I opened the door and struck a pose. "What do you think?"

"You look gorgeous! Lee, get up here and look at our gorgeous daughter!"

Mom walked in a few moments later and gasped dramatically.

"Stunning," she said. "Completely stunning."

I ran my hands down the front of the dress. It was unlike

anything I'd worn or owned and I had no idea what Ryan was going to think, but I liked the way I looked, so did it really matter?

Of course it mattered, I wanted her to think I was hot. Most compliments I got on my looks rarely used the word "sexy." I wanted her to think I was sexy.

I did have one issue when I turned around again and saw that I had a line from my underwear visible. My parents had left and gone back downstairs, so I just hauled the dress up and pulled off my underwear. There wasn't time to search for a pair that would work better. I'd just have to go without. Thankfully, the straps of the dress hid my bra, so that wasn't a concern.

I didn't have a coat that really went with the dress, but I grabbed my favorite leather jacket and called it good.

My hair went up and I slid in my favorite earrings and did a few things with makeup and I was good to go and downstairs waiting for Ryan when she pulled in.

This time, I didn't rush her out to the car. I waited and she knocked on the door. I pulled it open and savored the surprise on her face. Her mouth even dropped open as her eyes went wide. She clenched her jaw and I could barely concentrate.

"You look stunning," she said. "Completely stunning."

"So do you," I said, taking in her simple black suit with off-white shirt that was unbuttoned to reveal a delectable amount of clavicle.

"What a gorgeous couple," Mama said, and I whirled around to find my parents standing much closer than I thought they were.

"Can I get a picture?" Mama said, clasping her hands together. "Please?"

"Mama, I'm not going off to prom," I said, rolling my eyes.

"It's fine," Ryan said, putting her arm around me and

pulling me close. Mama grinned and pulled her phone out of her pocket to take a few shots.

"Okay, that's enough," I said after she'd taken at least five shots with two different poses.

"Have a good time, you two," Mama said.

"We'll bring you back some dessert," Ryan said, and Mama squealed.

"Drive safe," Mom said, giving Ryan a sharp look.

"This is ridiculous, bye," I said, tugging Ryan toward the door.

She laughed as we walked to the car.

"They really love you," she said as she opened the door.

"I'm fine with them loving me, it's the closeness and interfering that is a little much. Although, I have Mama to thank for this dress, so I guess I don't really have any reason to grumble," I said. I also needed to remember Ryan's rocky relationship with her parents. Not everyone was as lucky to have two loving parents like I was.

"I'll have to thank her," Ryan said, looking over at me. "It's a great dress."

"Thanks," I said, looking out the window. "So, where are we going?"

Ryan's lips formed a smirk. "You'll see."

"THIS DOESN'T LOOK LIKE A RESTAURANT," I said, feeling a little uneasy.

"I know," she said. "We're not at the restaurant yet."

It took a little bit to realize we were at a small airfield and across the pavement was an actual helicopter.

"Is that a helicopter?" I asked, which was a rhetorical question.

"Yes," Ryan said, looking over at me. "It's faster than driving."

"Hold up," I said, putting my hand up. "We're going to dinner in a helicopter?"

"Yes," she said. "Is that okay with you?"

I couldn't really process what was happening right now. She might as well have said we were hopping on a horse and riding to the restaurant.

"A helicopter," I said, one more time, just to be sure.

Ryan nodded. "A helicopter."

I stared at said helicopter and the people who were running around and prepping it, I assumed.

"I've never been on a helicopter before," I said.

"Scared?" she asked.

I glanced over at her. "No," I lied.

THE HELICOPTER RIDE was cramped and scary, but short. Ryan tried to point things out along the way, but every time I looked out the window, I was nauseated, so I stopped.

It was a relief when my feet were back on solid ground. This time we were at another airfield. Ryan led me toward a sleek black car with a man in a suit standing next to it. He opened the rear door for us.

"I feel like I'm on a TV show, or I won a contest," I said as I got in, sliding along the seat to the other side.

"Should I say hello to the driver?" I whispered to Ryan. I'd ridden in cars with a driver before, but not one as fancy as this.

"If you want," she whispered back.

"Hi," I said, my voice sounding too loud.

"Good evening," the driver said, taking us away from the airfield.

"Wow," I said softly to myself. This was something else.

WE ARRIVED at a restaurant that had been converted from an old mill, with a river and waterfall right next to it. The setting was rustic but refined.

Ryan led me to the entrance and was greeted warmly by a hostess who led us through the dining room and then up a set of stairs to the second floor. It looked like it was set up for an event, but no one else was here.

We followed her through a set of glass doors and onto the porch, which looked over the falls. There was one table set up for two already that she directed us toward.

"Wow," I said as I looked out at the view. The restaurant was so amazing that my anxiety was distracted. That had never happened before, but I was going to go with it.

"Can we have a moment?" Ryan asked the hostess as she filled our water glasses.

"Of course," she said. "I'll send your server up in a few minutes."

"Thank you," Ryan said, and then we were alone.

"I don't even know what to say," I said, gazing at Ryan. "This is incredible. I was not expecting anything like this."

"It's not too much? A lot of people would consider taking a helicopter to dinner a little too extravagant," she said, fiddling with her water glass.

"I mean, it's over the top, but in a good way," I said. "A very good way."

The rush of the water below us and the warm summer breeze only added to the beauty of the evening.

"I bet this place is gorgeous in the fall with the leaves changing on the trees," I said.

"It is. This is one of my favorite restaurants. I've even come here in the winter and eaten outside," she said.

I hadn't known that. She brought me to a place she loved and had created this beautiful time for us. This was a gift.

"Thank you for bringing me here," I said, reaching for her hand. Ryan squeezed me back.

"I hoped this would be okay since it was away from the other people and it would just be the two of us. I thought being outside would help too," she said. "Is it okay?"

"Honestly, this is the best I've felt in a restaurant in a long time. I wonder if this is what other people feel like," I said. Ryan stroked my hand with her fingers and a server said hello and stole our attention.

The menu was set, so we were both given a list of courses and a wine list. I chose my options and then the server disappeared again.

"I can't believe we took a helicopter here," I said. "My parents are not going to believe that."

"And we get to take a helicopter back," she said.

Our wine arrived and Ryan held up her glass.

"I'm not good at toasting. Do you have any suggestions?" she asked me.

"To relaxing," I said.

"Relaxing," she agreed as we tapped our glasses together.

"THIS IS BLOWING MY MIND," I said as the server took away our plates. "I feel like so much fancy food is like, one scallop on a piece of wilted lettuce with a smear of cranberry sauce or something, but this is good."

The food was both hearty and fresh and substantial. I was going to have to struggle to have room for dessert.

The wine that Ryan had picked out was excellent, and I was doing my best not to think about how much this evening was going to cost. Of course, Ryan had the money, but still.

"Uncle Mark is having a barbecue this weekend," she said as I tried not to lick my plate. I'd had the salmon and the sauce was so good I wanted to eat it with a spoon.

"Did you want to come?" she asked.

"Oh, uh…" I said.

Ryan put her fork down. She'd methodically demolished her strip steak with neat little bites. I wondered if she wanted to order another one.

"This is a completely no-pressure invitation. I just wanted you to know that you could come. It will just be Uncle Mark, Aunt Sadie, Layne, and Honor. Just family."

That didn't sound so bad. Definitely better than the pool party.

"Can I think about it and let you know later in the week when I see how I feel?" I asked.

"Of course," she said. "Think about it and let me know."

And that was that. No further pressure, no telling me it was all going to be fine, that I was being dramatic.

"I will," I said.

In addition to a slice of chocolate mousse cake, Ryan got us a cheese plate.

"What do you think your parents would like?" she asked me.

"Mama would kill me if I didn't bring the chocolate mousse cake, and Mom would want the cheesecake."

We ordered both of those to go, and I hoped they would be safe going on the helicopter.

Ryan sat back in her chair and looked out at the falls.

"I'm glad I could share this with you," she said.

"I'm glad you did," I said. "Now, is the helicopter on call all the time? Because it would be cool to have that for when the traffic is really bad."

She laughed.

"I'm not the president," she said. "But that would be cool."

I wanted to ask more questions about the helicopter situation, but I didn't want to dig too much or make her feel weird about it, so I didn't. Dessert arrived and I couldn't help myself from eating an entire piece of cake in a few bites.

"Do you want another?" Ryan asked.

"No," I said. "Definitely not. I think I'd explode."

"Are you sure?" she asked, and I bit my lip.

"Will you help me if I can't finish it?" I asked.

"I'll always help you finish," she said, leaning forward and winking.

All of a sudden, I wasn't as interested in the cake.

"Will you now?" I asked.

"Mmm," she said.

Even though I was thinking about Ryan more than the cake, I ate a second piece anyway, giving her a bite.

The server brought us a bag with the bonus desserts and told us to have a good night.

I watched her leave and looked over at Ryan.

"The bill is already taken care of," she said.

"Oh," I said. "I assumed. Thanks. That's really generous."

"I have money and I like spending it with you," she said, shrugging one shoulder. "You're helping me relax and figure out hobbies."

We had not talked about hobbies during this dinner, oops. I hoped I hadn't neglected my duties.

We headed back downstairs and got back into the car.

"Did the driver wait the whole time we were at dinner?" I asked her in a low voice.

"He's used to it," she said. "He's very well compensated. Very well."

The sun was setting by the time we got back in the helicopter, with me balancing the desserts on my lap, one of my hands gripping Ryan's when we took off and landed. Using a helicopter wasn't necessarily my favorite way to travel, but it did get you there fast. It would have taken hours to get from Arrowbridge to the restaurant. The helicopter got us there in a fraction of the time.

It was still a relief to get back into Ryan's car at the airfield. Maybe it was silly to trust her more than a trained helicopter pilot to get me safely home, but I did.

"That was an adventure," I said as we headed back to Arrowbridge.

"Good adventure?" Ryan asked.

"Hell yes," I told her.

She pulled into my driveway far too soon.

"My parents will be happy I'm in one piece," I said with a laugh. "They're not going to believe me when I tell them, but I have evidence." I'd taken more than a few selfies on the helicopter and then a few shots at the beautiful restaurant.

"Safe and sound," Ryan said, taking my hand and kissing the center of my palm.

"Safe and sound," I repeated.

Heat crackled between us and I wished, so much, that I didn't have to go to work tomorrow. All I wanted her to do was unzip my dress and discover that I wasn't wearing any bottoms under it.

Ryan made a frustrated sound. "Is it bad that I don't want you to go inside? I know you have to work tomorrow, but I wish tonight didn't have to be over."

"It doesn't have to be," I said. "Just give me like, five or ten minutes."

I dove forward and gave her the fastest kiss I could and then jumped out of the car. We'd only agreed to go to dinner, but I didn't want to just go to bed and read a book. I wasn't done with her yet.

"Hi, I'm going over to Ryan's," I called when I came through the door. I set the bag of extra desserts on the entry table and attempted to run up the stairs in the form-fitting dress. It didn't really work, even with the slit on the side, so I had to slow down and walk.

"What did you say, sweetie?" Mama called from the living room.

"I'm going over to Ryan's and I might stay the night. Just going to pack a few things."

I grabbed a tote bag and started chucking things in it, not even thinking what I was packing.

I made it down the stairs and found my parents poking in the bag I'd left.

"I'll tell you all about it tomorrow," I said, a little breathless. "I brought dessert, love you, bye."

Before they could even start to throw more questions at me, I was out the door and stumbling down the steps toward the car. I chucked my tote bag in the back and slammed my body down into the passenger seat.

"You didn't have to rush so much," Ryan said, looking at me with raised eyebrows.

"I know," I said, putting my hand on my chest to try and slow my breathing. Maybe I should start running regularly or something. "But if I lingered at all, my parents would grab me and want to know all the details and then I'd never get to see you naked tonight and that's kind of my top priority."

Ryan laughed. "I've told you that is a great dress, but I'm looking forward to seeing it on my floor."

"Hit the gas, Ryan," I said, snapping my fingers.

She did.

RYAN PICKED me up from the passenger seat and carried me into the house. For a moment, I remembered that this was the way that people were carried over the threshold after they got married. Silly, really, because Ryan and I were not getting married. Not even close to anything like that. She was my summer fling and right now all I wanted and needed was to be flung. Repeatedly.

Ryan set me down and stalked around me, looking for the zipper in the dress. I lifted my arm and started to slowly drag the zipper down my side. She stood in front of me, unmoving. As if she was mesmerized.

Once the zipper had been taken care of, I put my arms over my head.

"Help, I can't get it off on my own," I said, making my voice sound pathetic.

Ryan stepped right up to me, giving me a heated look.

"That's what she said," she murmured as she pulled the dress up and over my head, tossing it onto the floor. I'd wash it here on the gentle cycle before I gave it back to Mama.

Ryan let out a harsh breath when she looked down and saw that I wasn't wearing any bottoms.

"They didn't work with the dress," I said, trying to push her jacket off her arms.

"Stop," she said, and I did. "I need to—" she got on her knees, which made her only a few inches shorter than me.

"Oh, I like this," I said, stroking her hair.

"Get on the bed," she told me, and I backed toward the bed, with her following me on her knees. It was so fucking hot I could barely walk.

"Spread your legs for me, cupcake," she said, her voice low. I adored intense bedroom Ryan. She could also be playful and cute when it came to sex, but right now, she had a singular focus and it was me. It was overwhelming at times. This captivating woman who looked at me as if she was going to devour me from head to toe and I would beg her for more.

I climbed onto the bed and sat with my legs hanging over the edge, my thighs spread.

With a sound that was almost a growl, Ryan set my legs on

her shoulders and pushed me wider, leaving me completely open to her.

My body started shaking in anticipation of her. I propped myself on my elbows to watch her.

"Lay back," she said.

"I want to watch you," I said, our eyes meeting as she placed a fluttering kiss on the inside of my thigh. Since I had to use my arms to hold myself up, I couldn't touch her, and that was maddening. It was even more maddening when she blew a stream of air right over my center. I flinched and she set one hand on my hip, pressing me into the bed.

"You're going to be still for me," she said. "Can you do that?"

"Yes," I said, nodding. My blood raced even hotter and my legs started to shake with need.

"Good girl," she said, squeezing my hip. "No moving, or I'll stop."

"Okay," I said, transfixed by her.

She circled my clit with her tongue in a paralyzingly slow arc and both of my legs jumped. She stopped.

"I couldn't help that!" I moaned. "It's not my fault."

"Stay still," she said again.

"I'm trying," I said. "You're making it really hard."

She chuckled. "That's the point."

"Ryan, please."

She kissed the hood of my clit. "You can do it."

I made a frustrated sound but did my best to hold my body completely still. How I was supposed to do that with her going down on me was a fucking mystery, but I was hoping she'd give me some leeway.

Ryan fluttered her fingers at my entrance as she fluttered her tongue on my clit with the lightest touch and it was devastating, every time. How such a subtle thing could affect me so much, I didn't know, but she was an expert at it.

"You're so sweet, so good," she said to me and then slid two fingers inside. I was so wet that her hand made an indecent sound.

"Yes," I said, but right then I would have said yes to literally anything she asked me as long as she didn't stop again.

"You know," she said, working her fingers in and out of me, "I might have had more success with you being still if I'd brought out my rope, but I wanted you too badly to pull it out of the trunk and get you set up. Next time."

I whimpered at the idea of being tied to Ryan's bed. I'd never really done anything like that before and it was more exciting than I would have thought. Completely at Ryan's mercy as she pleasured me. I wanted that to happen.

"I love your sex trunk," I said, and she buried a laugh between my legs. I couldn't help but arch up against her. Ryan pulled away.

"Ryan! You're being an asshole! It's impossible to stay still when you're going down on me, so just make me come, please. It hurts."

The ache between my legs was all I could fucking think about and I needed release or else I was going to die. Probably.

Ryan sighed and then slid three fingers inside me in one smooth thrust.

"Oh, *fuck*," I moaned and then she attacked my clit. There was no other word for it. Her mouth was focused and intent on my pleasure as her fingers did their work on me inside. The combination had me shattering and screaming within seconds, so rocked by the intensity of the climax that threatened to permanently alter my body, or at least scramble my brain a little bit.

When I finally came down, I realized I was staring up at Ryan's ceiling. My arms had collapsed at some point and I'd fallen back.

"Holy fucking shit," I said, putting my hand on my heart. It was pounding so hard, she could probably see it.

The bed dipped as Ryan joined me, a grin on her face. She was still completely clothed, and the only way you could tell anything had happened was her messy face and her hair.

I patted her shoulder.

"Thank you," I said.

"You're welcome, cupcake," she said, taking my hand and kissing it. "I just couldn't help myself when you took off that dress."

"Give me like, two minutes and I am going to get that very nice suit off you and then it's payback time."

"Oh, is it?" she said.

"I'm so getting you back. Just you wait." I screwed up my face with determination.

Ryan laughed and kissed me. "You're adorable."

I grumbled until she started touching me again.

"SEX AND A HELICOPTER ride all in one day," I said, yawning as we lay in bed together. "It feels like years ago when I got up this morning and went to work."

And I would have to do it again way too soon, but I was trying not to think about that part. Sleep was for people who didn't get to have sex with six-foot-three goddesses.

"Do you get vacation days?" Ryan asked. The only light in the room came from the fireplace flickering over our skin.

"Just a few, but I don't like to take them and leave Sydney in the lurch," I said. "She trusts me and relies on me, and I want to be there for her. She gave me a chance when not a lot of people would."

My resume was one of those that was full of red flags, since I'd bounced around so many jobs, so many different jobs. I'd taken what I could, when I could, and had to leave a few times when my anxiety became too much. That had been the worst.

"I understand," she said. "I can see you when you're done with work, and there's always weekends. I just have to figure out what to do during those other forty hours."

I sat up. "We still haven't talked about hobbies, so let's come up with some stuff for you to try. You already know how to cook, so you don't need to do that."

Ryan thought for a moment. "I don't really know how to bake, though. Cooking requires a different instinct."

"Mama says the same thing," I said. "Okay, baking. That sounds fun. And, you hopefully get to eat delicious treats at the end of it."

"Hopefully," she said. "I do love watching those baking shows where they make the fancy little cakes and things filled with jam and cream. I should probably start with something simple. Like cupcakes." She reached over and spanked my ass. I yelped and then started laughing.

"As long as I get to try them," I said.

"I'll definitely save you one," she said, and then reached over to get her phone. "Help me find a recipe."

She searched online and scrolled slowly.

"Ohh, those lemon ones are pretty," I said, pointing.

"Lemon it is," she said, saving the link.

Chapter Eleven

"Did you sleep at all last night?" Sydney asked me the next day when I got to work. I was almost late due to needing to make out with Ryan before she dropped me off.

"Yes," I said, covering a yawn with my hand. "Sorry."

Sydney went to the little coffee area and plugged it in. "You're going to need this."

"Yes, I am," I said, even though I'd already had one cup with Ryan when she made me breakfast, but it wasn't making a dent in my tiredness yet.

"Did you stay up late reading again?" Sydney asked. That had happened to me a few times.

"Uh huh," I said, latching onto the excuse. "Really good book. *Really* good." I stretched my back and then smiled as she handed me a fresh cup of coffee.

"Since it's going to rain all day, things might be quiet, but you never know," Sydney said, flipping the Open sign and unlocking the door.

"Got it. I'm going to check the orders and start packing. Yell if you need me," I said.

"You got it," she said as the first few customers walked in.

WE'D GOTTEN SLAMMED with orders for some reason, so I spent most of my morning packing and checking my messages from Ryan. I was still tired as fuck, but that didn't matter so much. I was happy because I got to see Ryan after work. She'd sent me pictures of her baking process from going to the store to get the ingredients, to mixing it all and then decorating. She wouldn't show me the final product until I saw it in person after dinner. I felt guilty for not being home last night and having dinner with my parents, so I wanted to at least see them after work to fill them in on the helicopter dinner date and see how they were. Ryan had been completely understanding and fine about seeing me later and I couldn't put into words how good that made me feel. In the past, people had given me weird looks or made comments about how close I was with my parents. Ryan never did that. She listened as I told her about Mom and Mama and how much I adored them.

She really was great. Not just a hot piece of ass, although she was that, too.

"SWEETIE, it feels like we haven't seen you in a year," Mama said, throwing herself at me.

"Mama, it's been less than a day," I said, hugging her and then hugging Mom.

"Yes, but we want to hear all about your big date!" Mama said, dragging me into the kitchen. "Talk to me while I cook."

I tried to give them just the highlights, but they wanted to know everything, and it was fun to tell the two people I loved about my date. I guess it was a date, now that I thought about it.

"I see that look in your eyes, Lydia," Mom said. "Someone wants a helicopter date for our anniversary in August."

"I have no idea what you're talking about," Mama said, a gleam in her eyes.

"Can you get the number for the helicopter rental?" Mom stage-whispered to me.

I laughed. "I'll see what I can do."

"I PACKED up some leftovers for Ryan," Mama said, shoving a glass container at me. "I know you said she's a good cook, but I want to make sure she's eating, since you said she gets hungry all the time."

I took it and thanked her because fighting was completely useless. If Mama wanted to feed someone, she was going to do it.

This time I took my own car to Ryan's. I frowned as I started it up, remembering the sound of Ryan's car and how comfortable the seats were.

"Mama made you dinner," I said, holding the container out to her as she opened the door.

"Oh. I already ate," she said.

"She knows. You can heat it up later," I said.

She took it from me and stepped back to let me in.

"Tell her thank you for me," she said, putting the container in the fridge.

"I will," I said, looking at the beautiful display of cupcakes on the island. She'd found a tiered tray and had arranged them so they looked right out of a pastry shop.

"What is it?" she asked me when I turned to her.

"You're one of those people who's good at everything, aren't you?" I asked. "You're *that* girl."

Ryan rolled her eyes and crossed her arms. She had a black T-shirt and gray joggers on, as if she'd been working out. Hot.

"I'm not good at everything," Ryan said. "You never know, those cupcakes could taste terrible."

"They're not going to taste terrible," I said, reaching for one and pulling off the paper. Ryan drummed her fingers on the counter as she waited for me to take a bite.

Not only did the cupcake have a delectable lemon cake, it was topped with a meringue frosting and sprinkles. I took a bite and it melted in my mouth.

"Oh my god," I said, my mouth full. "This is soooo good."

Ryan's hands clenched. "Really?" she asked.

"Really times infinity," I said before taking another massive bite, almost devouring the entire thing. There was frosting on my nose, but I didn't care. I snagged another cupcake and Ryan selected one too.

"Okay, if you don't stop me, I'm not going to stop myself," I said, licking frosting from my thumb.

"You don't have to stop. You can have anything you want," Ryan said, swiping her finger at the corner of my mouth to catch a bit of frosting I'd missed.

Suddenly I wasn't thinking about cupcakes. I was thinking about all the wicked things that Ryan could do with her hands and her mouth.

"Anything?" I asked.

Ryan nodded. "Anything."

"I choose you and me minus clothes," I said, pointing between us.

"You can absolutely have that," Ryan said, pulling her shirt over her head.

RYAN READ some more of the book to me later. She seemed…satisfied. I couldn't put my finger on the subtle differences, but she was different as she told me about her cupcake adventures. She'd thrown away two previous batches before settling on the one that she gave me.

"See? I'm not good at everything," she said.

"You kind of are," I said. "But I'm learning to deal with it."

Ryan laughed and pulled me into her arms.

"I promise you, I'm not good at everything."

I wanted to argue with her, but she was warm and I needed snuggles.

"Are you going to bake again tomorrow?" I asked.

"I might. I was also thinking of spending it at the beach. I'd like to get in a good long swim and then maybe sleep. I can't remember the last time I just sat on the sand for a while. I'm usually in and out and I come home and shower. Going to try something different tomorrow," she said.

"You should look for a wishing rock," I said. Ryan's fingers stroked up and down my spine.

"What's a wishing rock?" she asked, and I told her.

"I'll find one," she said.

"You'll probably find dozens of them. You're bound to be good at finding wishing rocks."

"I'll do my best," she said. "I'll make sure I find a good one for you."

"No," I said, "the point of a wishing rock is to find one for your own wish."

"I'll have to figure out what to wish for," she murmured, and I could tell she was close to sleep, even though it was still early.

"That's up to you. It doesn't have to be a big wish. Sometimes even small wishes can change our lives."

She kissed forehead and I could tell she was smiling. "I don't have to wish for anything right now."

"Nothing? I could go for another cupcake that I don't have to get out of bed to get. That would be pretty great."

Ryan laughed. "I'll go get you one in a minute. How's that?"

I closed my eyes and sighed. "Works for me."

"I'VE GOT TO SAY, I really enjoy getting ready here," I said the next morning as I sat at the vanity and did my hair for the day. Ryan had gotten up before me and had already squeezed in a workout while I continued to sleep in her huge bed.

She grinned at me as she brushed her teeth.

I also loved making breakfast with her. At home, I usually ate whatever Mama made, but Ryan let me chop and fry things and even flip the pancakes. When I'd lived alone I'd eaten a lot of chicken strips and frozen waffles because cooking was so exhausting after dealing with my anxiety all day. I'd also ordered a fuckton of pizza.

"Lemon is a fruit, so really, this is fruit salad," I said when Ryan gave me a look for putting a cupcake on my plate.

"Uh uh," she said, picking up a slice of bacon.

We sipped our coffee and ate, and I absolutely did not want to go to work. So much had changed in such a short period of time.

"Have fun at the beach," I said, leaning over to give her a kiss as I got up from the table to put my dishes in the dishwasher.

"I'll try. Have a good day at work. There's a cupcake all packed up for you on the counter so you can take it with you," she said.

"Thanks," I said, taking the container and shoving it in my

bag. "See you later, Ryan."

"Bye, cupcake," she said, smiling at me from across the room.

~

"OKAY, WHAT IS GOING ON?" Sydney said when I got to work a few minutes early.

"What?" I asked, putting my bag in the back and shoving my lunch in the fridge. I'd made a sandwich at Ryan's and stole a bunch of snacks too, not to mention the cupcake I got to look forward to.

"Something is up with you. Something good. And I might think that you got a new moisturizer or something, but I'm guessing it has to do with a hot lady."

I let out a breath. My parents knew about Ryan, but it was different talking to a friend your age about something like this.

"I'm sort of dating someone? I mean, we're not dating, we're hanging out."

"Hanging out," Sydney said slowly, as if she was skeptical. "Is that what people are calling it now?"

I pulled up the new orders and started printing the shipping labels.

"I don't know what it is. All I know is that it's good. Really good."

Sydney grinned. "I fucking love this for you. Tell me everything." I followed her to the door so she could unlock it. No one was standing outside, so we had at least a few minutes for me to talk about Ryan.

"She's, um…" I trailed off, at a loss for words to describe Ryan. "She's tall. And sexy. And funny. She's good at everything. And I feel good around her," I said.

"Tall, you say?" Sydney said.

"Yes," I said slowly.

"Would her last name be Jewel, by any chance?" she asked.

Two people walked in just then and I smiled at her.

"I'm going to pack orders, talk later!" I called and scampered into the back.

"IT *IS* RYAN, I KNEW IT," Sydney said after those customers had left. "Layne is going to be thrilled."

"Is she?" I asked. "I'm definitely not good enough for her. She's so out of my league, I try not to think about it that much."

Sydney scoffed. "That's ridiculous. You're cute and fun and so sweet, Everly. You see people, and you care about them."

I couldn't stop myself from blushing.

"She's leaving, though. Her life isn't here. My life is here," I said. My new life.

"That doesn't mean you can't have a good time while she's here. Maybe that's what you both need. Just a sexy summer romance to blow off the cobwebs," she said, raising and lowering her eyebrows.

"I've never had a summer romance before," I said. "I don't really know what I'm doing."

Sydney squeezed my shoulder. "I've had lots of summer romances. I can be your summer romance Yoda. You've got this."

Sydney had a whole lot more confidence in me seeing this through than I did.

"I guess," I said. My phone went off with a message from Ryan. It was a picture of her holding up a rock with a perfect white ring around it.

Wishing rock? she asked.

It's perfect I responded.

Wish you were here with me she sent.

You're not supposed to tell anyone your wish, that way it won't come true I replied.

See? I'm not good at everything. I'm bad at wishing she sent.

"It seems to be going well," Sydney said, and I looked up from my phone. I'd almost completely forgot she was standing there.

"She's so intimidating," I said. "And not just because of being tall. She grew up going to a country club and she went to a fancy college and she knows how to hire a helicopter. I feel like we don't have anything in common," I said, voicing one of my biggest fears when it came to Ryan.

Sydney leaned against the wall.

"Do you have things to talk about? Like, is there a lot of awkward silence?" she asked.

"No," I said. "We have silence, but it's never awkward."

"Do you struggle to find something to say to her?"

I thought about that. "No."

"There you go. You could have a million things in common, but if you don't have that chemistry where you can talk, commonality isn't going to do shit," she said. "Lark and I don't seem like two people who could make a life together, but we're doing it. Love is just like that."

"We're not talking about love," I said.

"Right, but still. Chemistry. I saw it between the two of you at the pool party. The sparks were flying." She wiggled her fingers as if to demonstrate.

There was a crash and we both turned around to find Eileen looking surprised.

"It just jumped out of my hands," she said sadly as she looked down at the now-shattered platter.

"I've got this," I said, reaching for the broom. The bell over the door sounded and Sydney thanked me before heading out to handle the new customers.

"I don't know how it happens," Eileen said, still staring down at the platter.

"It's okay," I said, starting to sweep.

"Did I hear that you're dating someone?" she asked as I swept up. She got the dustpan for me.

"Oh, I'm not dating someone. I mean, I don't think I am. I'm not," I said. My face was getting red again.

Eileen blinked at me.

"Sounds complicated," she said.

"I don't think it's supposed to be." Flings weren't meant for complicated. Their very nature was to be easy and simple and fun. Easy, simple, fun. No one got their heart broken, no one cried at the end. You went off into the fall with good memories and a spring in your step and that was it. That was what I needed.

Eileen hummed to herself and I cleaned up the rest of the platter and went back to packing orders.

"HAVE you thought about the barbecue this weekend?" Ryan said to me that night.

"Oh, right." Why not? It was a casual thing with a small group of people I'd already met. It was also in a house I'd already been to. Plus, Ryan made me comfortable.

"Sure," I said. "I'm in."

She smiled. "Good. Then how about we have a little something to celebrate?" She pulled a box out of the fridge and flourished it at me. "I didn't make them, but I stopped by Sweet's and couldn't help myself."

"Show me, show me," I said.

Ryan opened the box and there were all manner of cupcakes inside. "I thought I could get some inspiration for what to bake next."

"What are they?" I asked and Ryan glanced into the box and then back at me.

"Honestly? I forget," she said with a laugh. "Let's figure it out."

She split each cupcake in half and we had a taste test.

"Okay, this one is definitely chocolate, obviously, but there's hazelnut? And maybe some raspberry?" I said.

Ryan nodded. "Definitely. There's a tiny little bit of saltiness too."

There was.

The two of us mowed down the cupcakes and then went for another walk, this time on the trail.

"This is really cool out here," I said, leaning down to gather some flowers.

"It is," she said. I heard a noise and looked to my left.

"Holy crap," I whispered as I watched the deer walk in between the trees.

"Wow," she breathed next to me. The deer's ears flicked around and then it looked right at us, freezing.

"Don't move," I said to Ryan. She held perfectly still, and I did as well. The deer watched us for a little while and then ran off, crashing through the brush.

"I feel like deer should be quieter when they move, but they're really loud," I said.

"Not as loud as moose," Ryan said.

"Have you ever seen a moose?" I asked.

She shook her head and I plucked another flower.

"Not a live one. I've seen a taxidermied one," she said. "It was bigger than you can imagine. Just when you think you've realized how big it is, you realize it's actually bigger."

"Yeah, I've seen video and I don't think I'd like to meet one in person," I said.

We walked to the end of the trail and turned around. I handed her the bouquet when we got closer to the house.

"Thank you," she said, taking it. "No one's ever given me flowers before."

"What do you mean?" I asked. "You mean no one's ever just gone out and picked some."

"No. No one has ever bought me flowers either," she said.

"Not from a store or for an award or anything?" I asked. It sounded impossible. Not even when she graduated?

Ryan held the front door open for me. "Never."

"Oh," I said. "Well, I'll bring you lots of flowers to make up for it."

For the first time, Ryan's face was fully blushing. "You don't have to do that."

"It's not that big a deal," I said. "There's lots and lots of flowers around here. If I'm already walking around, it's not that hard to bend down and grab a few."

"Still. Thank you." She fingered the petals of one of the flowers and then checked her phone.

Ryan frowned as she read the text message. "Hm."

"What is it?" I asked.

"Oh, it just looks like the barbecue is going to be bigger than I told you. Sydney and Lark are coming, and so are Joy and Ezra and then Lark's friend Mia and Layne's brother and his girlfriend. Oh, and the twins were supposed to be at a friend's house, but the other kids got sick, so they'll be there too. Are you good with that?" She looked up to see my reaction.

"Oh," I said, trying not to let my body react and failing. "That's a lot of people."

"It is. But everyone you've met before," she said in a careful voice.

"Yeah," I said, nodding. "You're right. I can do it."

"You sure?" she asked.

"I'm sure," I said, nodding and looking into her eyes. "I'm sure."

Chapter Twelve

PANIC HIT me the moment I woke up on Saturday and I didn't know why. I threw the covers off my sweating body and told myself to take a deep breath. I fucking hated this. I hated it so much. I reached for my water bottle and my medication, swallowing the pills as quickly as I could and laying there to wait for them to kick in.

I grabbed my phone to try and distract my brain, but it didn't work, so I forced myself to get up and get dressed in the outfit I'd picked out last night. Just in case I wanted to go in the pool, I put on my suit and another one of my caftans.

My face was pale in the mirror as I washed it and brushed my teeth before putting my hair up and then going downstairs. The barbecue wasn't for a few hours, but it was easier being ready ahead of time than having to scramble.

"You look gorgeous, sweetie," Mama said. "Do you think you can eat anything?"

"I can try some toast," I said, sitting down in the breakfast nook.

"Of course," Mama said, putting two slices in the toaster.

"Guess what we're doing today?" Mom said, sitting next to me.

"Going on a date?" I asked.

"Yes!" Mama said, raising her spatula in the air. "We are going to pick out a new tent and then for lunch and then I found this house showing that we're going to pretend we're rich so we can go see. It was owned by a relative of the Kennedy's, I heard."

"That sounds like a great day," I said. Not for the first time, I found myself jealous of my own parents. They were so in sync with each other. Each of them had their own hobbies and interests, but they meshed so well together. I thought again about what Sydney had said about how chemistry could overcome differences.

My parents had chemistry coming out their ears. Mom went over to Mama and pulled her into a dance hold, twirling her around the kitchen as she told the speakers to play the song they'd danced to at their wedding.

I watched them sway together, looking at each other as if they were the only two people in the world.

That. I wanted that. I ached for it so much I could barely breathe. The wanting was a good distraction from my anxiety, which was finally starting to subside a little with the distraction and the medication. I ended up getting my own toast so they could keep dancing together.

RYAN SENT me a text message to let me know she was coming over early to get me if that was okay. I told her it was fine and asked why.

Is it weird if I say I want to hang out with them? You talk about them so much I feel like I already know them so well she sent.

I stared at the message as my heart did something funny that had nothing to do with anxiety.

It's not weird at all I responded.

She showed up ten minutes later and I let her in.

"Hey," I said.

She pulled something from behind her back. It was a massive bouquet of pink and yellow and white flowers. She also had a bag in her hand.

"I didn't pick them, but they're still pretty," she said, almost apologetically.

"They're gorgeous, thank you," I said, taking them from her and walking toward the kitchen.

"Hello," Ryan said as Mom and Mama looked over as if they'd been having a whispered conversation and we'd just interrupted.

"Ryan, it's so nice to see you," Mama said, going over to give her a hug.

"Oh, uh, it's nice to see you," she said. "I brought you a little something."

"You didn't have to do that," Mama said, but she snatched the bag anyway.

"It's a dip set, and matching water bottles. I looked up what a good present for a gym teacher was," she said, the words coming out a little fast. Her shoulders were hunched, which didn't make her smaller but she was trying.

"This is beautiful, Ryan, thank you," Mama said, looking at the box with the dip set. "That was so thoughtful." Mama gave her another hug and Mom immediately went to the sink to wash her new water bottle out.

"I have wanted one of these things for ages, but I just couldn't bring myself to buy one. This is fantastic."

She filled it up with ice and put the top on.

"I'm going to make so much dip in this," Mama said, pulling the bowls out of the box.

"Good job," I whispered to Ryan.

"Thanks," she whispered back.

"Oh, I'm so sorry, the present made me forget my manners," Mama said. "Ryan, would you like some coffee or tea? I also have snacks." She started pulling things out of cupboards in a frenzy.

"Coffee would be great," Ryan said, looking at me.

"Coming right up," Mom said. "Please, sit down."

Ryan and I sat at the table in the breakfast nook. Ryan took up a lot of room, but I liked seeing her in my house.

"Any cream or sugar for your coffee, Ryan?" Mom asked as Mama fluttered around, making up a snack plate whether anyone wanted it or not.

"Black is fine," she said, and Mom brought it over to her.

"Thank you," Ryan said, taking it.

"Of course," Mom said. "Sweetie, anything for you?"

"Some tea, please. Ginger," I said.

Mom made the tea and Mama brought over a smorgasbord of things.

"This really is too much," Ryan said, her cheeks going pink.

"We love having guests," Mama said, beaming. "Next time I'll make you some dip and you can tell me which one you like best."

Ryan looked like she was going to protest, and I squeezed her shoulder as Mom set my tea on the table.

"Just let it happen," I said. "It's easier to just let it happen."

Ryan looked at me with a bewildered look on her face. Something told me her mother had never made her a snack plate. The nanny had probably done that. One of the nannies. Not that it was a bad thing, because Layne was a nanny and the kids she looked after loved her. They also had two parents who would drop anything for them, though, and who celebrated their accomplishments. And bought them flowers.

Ryan sipped her coffee and for the first time I could see she was nervous.

"Everly said you're visiting for the summer?" Mama asked, sitting with Mom across the table from us.

Ryan nodded and I nudged her under the table to elaborate. I was the one with diagnosed social anxiety, not her.

"Yes, I'm visiting family," she said. Okay, that wasn't great, but she was getting somewhere.

"She's staying in the most gorgeous house," I said. "It's off Black Bear Lane, down a private road."

"Oh, I know that place. It's gorgeous," Mama said. "Not a bad house to spend your summer in."

"No, it's not," Ryan said. "I tried to find another rental, but this place is owned by a friend of my parents."

That made sense. She hadn't told me that.

"You know, if you're looking to go somewhere different, I would be more than happy to show you what we have, in all price ranges."

"Mama! Are you pitching her?" I asked.

"Of course not, I was just offering," she said, and Ryan looked back and forth between us.

"You are shameless," I said, narrowing my eyes at her as she widened them innocently. "You're just using me to get a commission. I feel so used."

"ABC, sweetie. Always Be Closing," she said with a smile.

"You are shameless," Mom said with a laugh.

"You love it when I'm shameless," Mama said, reaching for Mom's hand and then leaning over to kiss her.

"I am begging you not to make out in front of me and Ryan right now," I said.

"We're not making out," Mom said, tearing her attention away from Mama. "Everly, why don't you give Ryan a tour?"

"Uh, yeah, sure," I said, getting up. "You want a tour?"

"Of course," Ryan said, rising to her feet. "Thank you so

much for the coffee and the food." She hadn't touched any of the snacks, so I'd have to talk to her about that when we were alone because if she didn't eat something, Mama was going to think that it was something she'd done and I would never hear the end of it.

I took Ryan around the downstairs and then pretty much skipped the second floor and took her to the third.

"This is pretty much all mine," I said. "Perks of being an only child."

My room was a little messy, but there was no dirty laundry on the floor or anything embarrassing left out.

Ryan looked around the room and I waited to hear what she thought. She walked by the bed and looked at a framed picture of me and my parents on vacation together from a few years ago.

"This room looks like you," she said finally, facing me.

"Does it?" I asked. I had picked out everything in here and decorated it the way I wanted with lots of color and chaos and fun.

"Your family is great," she said, sitting down on my bed.

"I'm sorry if Mama was being a little weird about the house thing. She can't turn her realtor brain off," I said, joining her.

Ryan shook her head as she stared out my window. "No, it's fine. I might actually want to find somewhere else. It feels too empty for just me," she said.

"Yeah, I could see that. This house always feels weird when it's just me. I love it during the day but at night it makes me nervous," I said.

She was quiet for a while and I was dying to know what was on her mind.

"Your family is wonderful, Everly," she said, and I realized there was a tear drifting down her cheek.

"Ryan?" I asked, "what is it?"

She sniffed and wiped her face. "Nothing. It's nothing." She still wouldn't look at me. I used her chin to turn her head.

"Talk to me," I said.

She took a shaky breath and looked up at the ceiling, as if she was trying to compose herself.

"Your parents love you," she said in a soft voice. "They love you and they love each other."

"I know," I said.

"I don't know why this is happening," she said, sniffing again and swiping at her eyes.

"Hey, it's okay," I said, putting my arms around her. "You're allowed to have emotions and you're allowed to cry."

Ryan pulled me closer, hugging me so tight it was hard to breathe, but I knew that was what she needed. She might be nearly forty, but those hurts parents inflicted on you for decades didn't go away just because you were an adult.

"I'm sorry," she said, her voice muffled.

"You don't have to be sorry. You can feel however you want with me and I won't judge you. I can't judge anyone when I've literally had a panic attack at the thought of going to a new grocery store." So embarrassing.

I moved my hands up and down her back, trying to soothe her.

"I don't know how my life got like this," she eventually said, pulling back and gazing at me with reddened eyes. "I don't even know what I'm doing anymore, Everly. And I hate it."

"You're in luck. I don't know what I'm doing either." I reached over to my nightstand and got a box of tissues. She took one from me and blew her nose.

"Do you ever feel like a complete failure?" she asked with a little laugh.

"All the fucking time," I said. "For real. All the time."

Ryan let out a sigh. "My life doesn't look the way I thought it was going to, but I don't know what it should look like."

"Same," I said. "I never thought I would still be living at home, working at a pottery studio. But at least I'm not trapped in an apartment and not talking to other humans and scared to go outside anymore. This is a step up."

Ryan pressed her lips together and looked down at her hands.

"I'm sorry I'm such a mess. This isn't the Ryan that I show anyone," she said, rolling her shoulders back.

"I know," I said. "You see the Everly I don't show other people. Well, except my parents."

"I hate this, Everly. I hate it," she said. "I need to get my shit together."

"Tomorrow. You can get your shit together tomorrow," I said, reaching for her hands. "Today we're going to go to the barbecue and eat good food and get some sun and not worry about it."

She squeezed my hands. "So young, so wise."

I rolled my eyes. "I'm not that young, Ryan." She seemed to make a decision and got to her feet, pulling me with her.

"Come on, let's go."

WE WENT BACK DOWNSTAIRS and I grabbed my bag.

"Oh, I have a question for you, Ryan," Mama said. "I'm not sure if you have any way to check, but there was this candle that your company made and they discontinued it and I was just wondering—ouch!" She stopped speaking when Mom had obviously given her arm a little squeeze.

"You two have a good time," Mom said with a pointed look at Mama.

I grabbed Ryan's hand and started towing her out the door. "Love you, bye!"

"Oh, okay," Mama said, heaving a heavy sigh. "Have fun! It's called Fall Frolic, if you can check for me. I'll pay!"

I shut the door and looked at Ryan. She was trying to hide a smile.

"How long has she been waiting to ask me about the candles?" she asked.

"She's mentioned it a few times," I said. "You don't have to do anything. She'll get over it."

"No, I can check for her. She said Fall Frolic?" Ryan pulled out her phone and made a note and I couldn't stop myself from yanking her head down to mine to kiss her.

"What was that for?" she asked.

"No reason," I told her.

"THIS SEEMS LIKE A LOT OF CARS," I said as we reached Mark's house.

"I think a lot more people invited themselves than they expected," Ryan said as she parked her car.

"Great," I said. "Fantastic."

Ryan turned the car off and looked at me.

"I can take you anywhere else you want to go. We could go home, and I can talk to your mama about candles, or we could go to my place. If this isn't for you today, I support you."

I leaned over and kissed her. "I'm okay. How about we come up with a word that I can say and if I say it, you'll take me somewhere quiet?"

"Kind of like a safeword," she said.

"Right. Okay, now to come up with a word that wouldn't sound weird if I just dropped it in conversation."

"How about…how about if you say you want another negroni? That's normal," she said.

"Hey, that works. Let's go with that."

I put my hand on the door and pushed it open. Ryan joined me and then I realized that people were going to ask questions about us going in together.

"What are we telling people?" I asked, grabbing her arm. "About you and me, what are we telling people? I know we haven't talked about anything, so I don't want to have that conversation right now, but I just need to know what you want to do."

Ryan put both hands on my shoulders.

"It's okay. We're friends, right? I mean, we can tell them we're friends and that's all anyone needs to know."

Friends. The word stuck my throat and normally I wouldn't have minded it at all, and it was a good answer. If we said anything else, people would have more questions that neither of us could answer.

"Friends," I finally said, hating the taste of the word in my mouth. "Friends is good."

∼

"I'M SO glad you're here," Layne said. "Both of you."

"Me too," I said. There were three times as many people as I thought were going to be here and I was doing my best not to fall off a mental cliff. It was only Ryan's looming presence next to me, her body almost up against mine that kept me from completely crumbling.

"Help yourself to food and drinks and hop in the pool and have a brownie," Layne said as someone else came over to say hello.

"Thanks," I said and then I shared a look with Ryan. "Shall we get food?"

"If you're up for it," she said.

"I am," I said, giving her the best smile I could manage. Ryan put her hand on the small of my back and guided me toward the food table. Mark was at the grill and he gave Ryan a huge hug and called the twins over. They left a group of other kids and ran to come give Ryan hugs.

"Auntie R, will we be as tall as you?" one of them asked.

Ryan leaned down so she was closer to their eye level. "Only if you eat your vegetables and listen to your parents and get really good grades."

The twins rolled their eyes in perfect unison.

"Auntie R, we're too old to believe that," one twin said.

"Thanks for trying," Mark said with a laugh as he added some fresh burgers to the grill. "The older they get, the harder it is to lie about things."

"You're not supposed to lie," the girls said at the same time. They might wear different clothes and hairstyles, but other than that, they were so in sync. I wondered what that was like.

"I don't know how tall you're going to be, but there's a good chance, since both your parents are relatively tall, that you will be too. Have you learned about genetics yet in school?"

They shook their heads.

"You will," Ryan said. "For now, don't worry about being tall. There's nothing you can do about it anyway. You can be in charge of your clothes and your grades and how you treat others. Okay?"

They nodded in unison and she smiled.

"You're my favorite nieces," she said.

"We're your cousins," one of the twins said.

"I'm your aunt in spirit," she said. "Does that work for you?"

They both hugged her and then ran off to their friends.

"Monsters," she said fondly. "Sorry, I should have introduced you."

"I've met them," I said as we moved closer to the food table and Ryan got me a plate. "They're good kids."

"They are. I have the feeling they're going to be terrors as teenagers, so I'm trying to prepare now." She loaded up her plate and I took a few things here and there just to be careful. My plan was to nibble and hope my stomach behaved itself.

"They really look up to you," I said.

"Hopefully they'll learn from my mistakes," she said. "Let's find somewhere to sit. I hate eating standing up."

We sat at a small table together and Ryan demolished two cheeseburgers and a hot dog and then a massive amount of potato salad.

"I missed out on a lot of their life and I feel bad about that," Ryan said, looking over at the twins as they splashed in the pool with their friends, having chicken fights and screaming when someone lost.

"That's not your fault," I said, "you were living in another state and working."

"I know, but still," she said. "Uncle Mark is kind of the black sheep of the family. Let me tell you, family gatherings are more than tense. I avoid them as much as I can."

"Understandable," I said. "What was it like working for your family?"

Ryan shuddered. "It was… I hated it." She sagged in her chair and then shook her head. "I don't want to talk about it."

That was fair enough. This wasn't the right venue for having deep conversations about family drama.

Sydney came over with Lark and sat down with us. Mia arrived a few minutes later and also joined our table, which was pretty crowded, but I got shoved right next to Ryan, so I wasn't complaining.

"You can absolutely have some of our damages and mistakes," Sydney said to Mia.

"You don't have to do that," Mia said. "I can buy my own dishes and coffee mugs."

"Mia's moving into the apartment next door to us," Sydney

explained. "So I am probably never going to see my girlfriend ever again."

Lark rolled her eyes. "That's not true. I'll come home for… certain things."

Sydney raised her eyebrow. "Ohhh, I love certain things."

"Anyway," Mia said loudly. "I don't need any donations." Her face went red, betraying her lie. "I'm just glad to be getting out of my parent's house. Excited to walk around in my underwear."

Ryan leaned over and said in my ear "I'd like to see you in your underwear later. In even less."

I let out a little squeaking noise and everyone looked at me.

"Sorry," I said, slapping at my neck. "Bug bite."

"HOW ARE YOU DOING?" Ryan asked me later as we hung on the edge of the pool. The younger kids had gone inside to watch a movie for some reason, even though it was still gorgeous outside.

"I'm good," I told her, lazily kicking my feet. "Really. I am."

"Good," she said. "Whenever you want to go, we can go."

I closed my eyes and then sunk below the water and came up to find her waiting for me.

"You look like a mermaid," she said, pushing my hair back.

"Are you dating?" a voice said, making both of us turn.

"What?" I said, looking up into the faces of the twins.

"Are you dating?" they asked in unison.

"That's a rude question to ask," Ryan said. "You know you shouldn't ask people that."

The twins had a silent conversation with their eyes.

"Well?"

"Are you?"

"Go back to your friends or I'm going to drag you in here. Both of you," Ryan said, pointing at each one in turn. "Don't mess with Auntie R."

The twins crossed their arms and stood their ground until Ryan started to lunge out of the pool and then they screamed and ran back inside.

Ryan laughed. "Monsters."

∼

THE PARTY STARTED to wind down and one minute I was fine and the next I felt myself hit a wall.

"Hey, I need another negroni," I told Ryan as we sat together. I'd been talking with Sadie and two of her friends whose names I couldn't remember.

"Oh," Ryan said, meeting my eyes. "I would, but I really need to get home."

"Right, right," I said. "Well, we should get going."

We both got to our feet and made our goodbyes and headed to the car. I let out a huge exhale when I shut the door.

"Oh thank god," I said, leaning back in the passenger seat and closing my eyes.

"What do you need?" Ryan asked.

"Silence," I said and then she didn't say anything, so I opened my eyes and looked over at her. Ryan turned the car on and pulled out of her parking space. After a few minutes of her driving, I realized I hadn't told her where to go, but speaking just seemed like so much work. We'd planned to go back to her place and have me spend the rest of the weekend, but she was going in the direction of my parent's house.

"Your house," I finally said. "Go to yours."

She pulled into some random driveway and turned around.

∼

ONCE WE GOT to Ryan's, I could tell she wasn't sure what to do with me. I went right to the living room and sat on the couch and sent her a message.

I just need a few minutes to decompress. I'll be fine in a few I sent.

She read the message and then responded.

Is there anything I can do to help? she replied.

Do whatever you need to do. I'm just going to watch a show I sent.

Got it. If you need a snack or anything, let me know she responded.

I couldn't help but smile at the way she was being so gentle with me. I turned on the TV and found one of my old comfort shows and selected a random episode and wrapped myself completely in a blanket that I pulled off the back of the couch. Ryan moved quietly around the kitchen, but the sound didn't bother me. My body started to relax and before I knew it, I was falling asleep.

A DELICIOUS SMELL woke me up a while later.

"I fell asleep," I announced.

"You did," said Ryan, coming down the hallway. "Does that normally happen?"

"No," I said, sitting up and stretching my arms. "No, it doesn't."

She came over to sit with me. "How are you feeling?"

"Better," I said. "My battery is officially reset."

"Are you up for a cupcake?" she asked.

"Absolutely," I said, yawning. She started to get up, but I grabbed her arm.

"Thank you. For understanding and not getting mad that I was ignoring you. I know it doesn't make a lot of sense, but I've worked really hard to listen to my body and my brain and figure out what I need instead of ignoring it and then having a breakdown or panic attack."

Ryan took both of my hands. "It's okay, Everly. I know you weren't ignoring me, and I don't want you to ever feel like you can't tell me what you need."

Her thumbs made soothing circles on the backs of my hands.

"Seriously, though. Thank you," I said. "It means a lot."

Before I knew it, hot tears dripped down my cheeks and Ryan was pulling me into her arms.

"It's okay, shhhh, it's okay," she said, holding me.

"I'm sorry," I said. "I didn't plan for both of us to cry today."

She laughed and I sat back, wiping my face.

"Let me get you a tissue."

~

"I WOULD HAVE DECORATED them with candy hummingbirds, but I don't have the skills to make those," she said as she presented me with the cupcakes.

"You made hummingbird cupcakes," I said, remembering that she'd told me about her grandmother who'd made hummingbird cake.

"I did. They're probably garbage, but there's only one way to find out," she said, pushing one toward me. Each one had cream cheese frosting and a candied pecan on top.

"Cheers," I said, holding my cupcake up and she touched mine with hers.

The cake part was filled with fruit and pecans and balanced perfectly with the frosting.

"This is even better than your lemon ones," I said.

"Really?" she asked. "You don't think it's too..." Ryan trailed off, searching for something wrong with the cupcakes.

"They're perfect," I said. "Wouldn't change a thing."

She smiled and took another bite.

WE WENT on a walk post-cupcake and this time, Ryan picked the flowers. She'd been quiet for the rest of the day, but I decided to let her be.

"My dad wants me to come back to the company," she said. "He's been sending me countless emails about it."

"Oh," I said, my stomach sinking. "Have you talked to him?"

"No," she said, viciously yanking a flower out of the ground. "He keeps telling me that it's my legacy and that I'm his only child and I'm betraying the family and I just—"

I reached for her hand that was crushing the flowers in her fist.

"Hey," I said, "don't take it out on the flowers."

She let me take them and stood there, her jaw clenched as she started out into the distance.

"It wasn't the work, Everly. It wasn't the job itself. That was fine. It was everything else. No one would talk to me because they were afraid I'd snitch on them to my father, and everyone said yes to anything I said because they were afraid of me. It was miserable. I felt like I was in a cage every day and I just couldn't take it anymore. I couldn't wake up and do one more minute, let alone the rest of my life. And I know, I know that people would say that I'm just a spoiled little rich girl with rich girl problems, but I didn't want that life anymore." She'd been pacing around in a circle as she spoke and I let her get it all out.

"I didn't want that life anymore," she said, letting out a frustrated breath.

"I know exactly what you mean, and it doesn't make you a bad person. You don't have to live the life that was planned for you and that doesn't make you a bad person. You can say 'fuck it' and do what you want."

Ryan let out a laugh. "What the fuck do I want, though?"

I held my spare hand out to her. "Let's figure it out."

"YOU SHOULD TALK TO HONOR," I told her a while later as we made dinner together.

"Should I?" she said as she sliced peaches for a salad. She'd put some steak on the grill and was going to add the peaches to sear them. I was in charge of assembling the arugula and crumbling the bleu cheese on top, which was the easiest part of the job, but I wasn't complaining. Ryan on the grill was sexy as hell.

"Yeah. Her mom had lots of plans for her and she followed them, like you, until she couldn't take it anymore," I said, pouring the washed arugula from the salad spinner into a huge bowl.

"You mean when she met Layne?" Ryan said, taking the peaches and heading out to the grill. I followed her.

"Layne was the catalyst, but something else would have happened eventually. You had your own catalyst," I said.

Ryan snorted as she placed the peaches on the grill. "Layne told you about my ex, didn't she?"

"She might have mentioned it," I said, sitting in one of the comfy chairs.

Ryan set her tongs down and sat next to me.

"My parents kind of set us up, and I resisted at first, but she was beautiful and I thought we clicked. Both our families put a massive amount of pressure on us, and it just sort of happened. Before I knew it, we were engaged and planning the wedding of the century. One night, about two weeks before the wedding, she came to me in tears and told me that she couldn't go through with it. I was completely in shock, but I think I took it better than my parents. They were devastated and begged me to do what I could to get her back. I tried, but she had already moved on. She eloped with one of our friends a few months later, and the day after I found out, I quit my job."

"That fucking sucks," I said, and she let out a little laugh.

"It did fucking suck. The worst part is that I don't know if I really even loved her. We lived together, but we barely talked. She spent so much time at work or doing other things. We didn't do things together. We definitely didn't talk about anything serious. Now I don't even know what was keeping us together."

Ryan pulled the food off the grill and we assembled the salad.

"How am I doing at scattering the cheese crumbles?" I asked.

"Amazing," Ryan said, stifling a laugh. "Excellent scattering. Almost too good to eat."

"Almost," I said.

We sat down to eat, and Ryan poured me some wine.

"This is really expensive wine, isn't it?" I asked.

"It came with the house. There's a wine cellar in the basement," she said.

"Of course there is," I said. "This house has wine cellar energy."

Ryan snorted. "I can get a different house if you don't like this one."

"Ryan," I said. "You don't have to get a different house for me. Get one if you want to."

"I might. Maybe I'll rent a new one each week and find out

what I like." She said it so nonchalantly.

"Go for it," I said. "Why not?"

"You're right," she said. "Did you have anything in particular you wanted to do tomorrow?"

"Other than sex, I'm open for anything," I said.

"Good. I only have one other question: do you get seasick?" she asked.

I sipped my wine. "I don't think so? But you never know."

"We can stop and get something on the way," she said.

"On the way to…" I said, hoping she would elaborate.

"On the way to where we're going," she said with a satisfied smile.

"That's what you said when we went on the helicopter date," I said.

"There's no helicopter involved this time," she said. "But I still think you're going to like it."

"Color me intrigued," I said.

"YOU MAKE ME FEEL LAZY," I said the next morning when Ryan came back into the bedroom from her post-run shower.

"You could get up and run with me," she said, dropping her towel.

"I prefer more horizontal exercise," I said, sitting up and letting the blanket fall. My sleep shirt was so thin that you could see my nipples right through it, which was the point. Sleeping naked wasn't comfortable for me, but I liked giving Ryan a reason to touch me in the morning.

Ryan stared openly at me and I crooked my finger at her.

She approached the bed and leaned down to my level.

"What kind of horizontal exercise did you have in mind?" she asked.

"Oh, I had some idea of you," I said, reaching to stroke her center, "and me." I brushed my fingers across my lips.

"I think I like this idea," she said, crawling onto the bed with me.

"You know I want you to sit on my face, right?" I said and she laughed as she kissed me.

"Yes, I got the gist," she said, pushing me onto my back and taking my glasses off my face.

Chapter Thirteen

WE DIDN'T DRIVE to an airfield this time, but I wasn't disappointed when I saw the destination.

"Are we for real going on a whale watch?" I asked, after reading the sign on the small building situated in front of a dock that led down to the sparkling ocean and a lovely passenger boat.

"We are," Ryan said. "Let's take our motion sickness pills now."

She and I tossed back pills with some water and then made our way into the building.

Ryan checked us in while I looked at the pictures of gorgeous whales flipping in the ocean that other whale watchers had taken. In spite of living in New England my whole life, I'd never been on a whale watch before.

Ryan came back over and told me that we were checked in and could go down to the boat.

"Are we going to need those?" I asked, pointing to a picture of a family wearing plastic ponchos and smiling.

"They have them on the boat if we need them," she said, holding out her hand.

I took it and she led me down the steps to the dock.

A perky woman wearing a polo with the name of the company on it came over to us.

"You must be Ryan and Everly," she said, shaking both our hands. "I'm Jen and I'll be your guide for the trip. If you'll just watch your step."

Ryan and I got on the boat and I looked around, only seeing other employees and polo shirts aboard.

"Are we early?" I asked.

"It's a private tour," Ryan said, squeezing my hand. "That way you can see the whales and not have to deal with any puking children."

"Seriously?" I asked.

"It's just you and me," she said, gesturing to the boat. It could easily fit fifty or more people aboard, but it was just us and the crew, who were bustling about and getting everything ready.

Ryan smiled at me and I threw myself into her arms. She laughed and spun me around before setting me back on my feet.

"I knew you'd like that," she said.

"I love it," I said. "I absolutely love it."

WE GOT OUR PONCHOS, and Jen stood right next to us to give her talk as the boat cut through the ocean waves and the sun beamed down on us.

The motion sickness medication was doing its job and Ryan's arms were around me the whole time. All that was missing were whales.

As soon as I had the thought, I saw something to my right that looked like something. Moments later a tail flipped out of the water and then slid below the waves.

"If we're lucky, she might surface again. Based on the markings on her tail, that was Mrs. Bubbles. She got that name from a contest we had with the local schools," Jen said as Ryan and I laughed at the silly name.

I made sure I had my phone ready to video so I'd have some record that I'd seen a whale in person.

"There she is," Jen said as the whale broke the surface again, this time spinning vertically, her flippers flying as if she was dancing. The resulting splash was loud, and my mind couldn't comprehend her size. It was a relief we weren't closer.

"Wow," I said as the waves started tossing the boat. Ryan held onto me, keeping me steady.

"Incredible," she said in my ear.

"SOME DAYS we come out and we don't have any sightings, which can be a huge disappointment, but you hit the jackpot today," Jen told us after we'd seen two more whales (Takeshi and Nico).

"We'll take you over to where the seals hang out and then we'll turn around and head back," she said. "Do you have any questions?"

I shook my head. Jen was remarkably knowledgeable about whales, and kept her energy up the whole time, even though she must give this same speech every single day.

"Awesome, I'm just going to check on a few things and I'll be right back." She bounced off and Ryan pulled me closer.

"How much coffee do you think she drinks?" Ryan asked, and I turned in her arms so I could look at her.

"Way too much," I said. "But she's nice."

"She is," Ryan said. "Not as nice as you."

"But she does know more about whales," I said.

"I think I can live without the whale facts if I get to have you," Ryan said, kissing me. The boat made a huge dip and if Ryan hadn't been holding onto me, I would have definitely been on the floor of the boat.

"I've got you," she said, pressing her forehead to mine. "I've got you, cupcake."

"Thanks," I said. "This has been amazing."

"Are you hungry?" she asked.

"If they have food," I said. "It's probably only chips or granola bars or something."

Ryan grinned. "I think we can do better than that."

She led me back inside the covered part of the boat, which had lots of seating and was protected from both the sun and the water. I was a little lightheaded and realized I really was starving. I'd been too distracted by the whales to notice.

Ryan sat down at a table and one of the polo-shirted employees came right over and handed us menus.

"Can I get you started with some drinks?" he said, and I wondered how young he was. He didn't look over sixteen and was obviously eager to do a good job. Cute.

"We brought our own champagne, it should be on the boat," Ryan said.

"You think of everything," I said.

"I do my best," she said.

"Can I also get a water too?" I asked the server, and he gave me an enthusiastic nod before rushing off to find the champagne.

"Wow, they have a lot of options for a boat," I said.

"The food is probably just heated up below and not cooked fresh, but it's better than chips and granola bars," Ryan said.

The server came back with the iced champagne bottle and gave it to us, along with two cups.

"We can't use glass, you know," he said as if in apology.

"Of course," Ryan said, taking the bottle from him. "I've got this."

He seemed grateful as she expertly popped the top and poured some in each cup for us.

We ordered and the server dashed off again.

"You'd better tip him really well," I said.

"I will, don't worry," she said.

"To whales," I said, raising my cup.

"To whales, and to private whale watches," Ryan said.

"I think I like them better than helicopters," I said after taking a sip of the bubbling champagne. I wasn't going to ask how much it cost, but I recognized the name on the bottle as one that wealthy people drank.

Every now and then I would forget that Ryan was wealthy and then moments like this would remind me.

"I'll just have to take you on more helicopter rides so you can compare with a larger sample," she said.

"I'm up for that," I said. "I am so up for that."

THE FOOD WAS hot and surprisingly good and tasted amazing after being out on the ocean.

"It feels appropriate to be eating seafood while we're at sea," I said, finishing my shrimp scampi.

"It does, doesn't it?" Ryan said. "I know all our other dates have been surprises, but if there was something you wanted to do, I'm probably up for it."

I set my fork down and leaned back in my seat. "This is a date?"

Ryan nodded. "Yes, Everly, this is a date. What else would it be?"

I threw my hands up in the air. "I don't know! We've never talked about it. I didn't want to mess anything up by saying something."

Ryan looked at me as if I'd sprouted flippers myself.

"Everly," she said, putting her fork down and reaching for my hand. "We're dating. I know we haven't talked about it in those terms, but I'm not scared."

"Oh," I said. "I just figured since we hadn't talked, and you had that whole thing with your engagement, I just didn't know."

Ryan squeezed my hand.

"I'm sorry for not bringing it up. I thought maybe it would put too much pressure on you. That was my mistake," she said.

"What I'm hearing is that we're both not very good at this," I said with a laugh.

"Clearly," she said. "The last person I dated was set up for me years ago by my parents." Ryan made a face.

"I'm so glad my parents have never tried to set me up. Although, if they had known you, they would have set you up with me. You're quite the catch, Ryan."

She was more than a catch. She was the record-breaking fish that went viral because it was so huge.

"Good to know," she said. "And I think you're better at this than you think."

"That's very nice of you to say," I said. Now didn't seem like the time to bring up that I'd barely dated anyone before, so I didn't tell her. Besides, dating was just that: dating. Dating for the summer, a thing that lots of normal people did. This didn't have to be more than that. She wasn't ready for commitment, as much as she said she wasn't scared. Plus, she had a life to figure out and that wasn't going to end up in Arrowbridge. Ryan had bigger and better things in store for her than me.

"What are you thinking about?" Ryan asked.

I picked up my champagne and finished it. "Whales," I said.

"A PRIVATE WHALE WATCH SOUNDS AMAZING," Sydney said. "That's actually not a bad gift."

"I think it was really expensive," I said as we pulled coffee mugs to replenish the stock at Common Grounds, one of the shops where we sold on commission.

"Oh, I'm sure. Ryan has money to burn," Sydney said, checking her list.

"I try not to think about it too much," I said.

"Why not? If she's going to spend it, might as well have her spend it on you," she said. "Live it up."

"I mean, I kind of am," I said. "I feel like I shouldn't enjoy it as much as I do."

Sydney scoffed. "That's bullshit. Spend that money, my friend. Enjoy yourself."

"I'm working on it," I said.

"HEY," I said to Mia as I stepped up to the counter of the coffee shop. Normally I saw Lark, but she must have been on her break.

"Hey, nice to see you," she said, giving me a sweet smile. Her red hair was in a long braid today, with little tendrils curling around her face.

"I've got new mugs," I said, pointing to my car in the parking lot.

"Oh, of course," Mia said, her face getting red. She went over to the back and stuck her head into the office. "Hey, Liam, can you give Everly a hand with the mugs?"

Layne's brother, Liam, came out and gave me a big smile.

"Hey, Everly, how's it going?"

"It's going," I said, which made him laugh.

"Hey, that's good," he said, and we headed out to my car. Liam took the biggest box and I carried the second one, holding my breath so I didn't drop anything. Sydney wouldn't fire me for dropping a box of mugs, but I wanted to be extra careful anyway. Eileen worked hard to make each one by hand, and I knew the labor that went into them.

Liam and I brought the mugs into the back and I checked on the stock and replenished and rearranged the display.

"Hey, how's it going?" Lark said, coming back from her break and standing next to me at the display.

"Good, it's going. How are you?" I asked.

"It's going," she said with a laugh. "Sydney told me you and Ryan went on a private whale watch yesterday?"

I showed her some pictures as I told her about it.

"That is really cool," Lark said, and Mia leaned over the counter.

"Hey, can you cover me for my fifteen?" she asked.

"You got it," Lark said. "Duty calls."

I finished up and was looking at the drink menu when a woman with honey-blonde hair approached the counter.

"This isn't a caramel macchiato," she said, setting a cup on the counter. The only thing left in it was ice. "I'd like a replacement."

"If you knew it wasn't a caramel macchiato, then why did you drink the entire thing?" Mia asked, her voice sharper than the edge of a knife. I'd never heard her speak like that before. Being a barista couldn't be easy. She probably dealt with assholes all day every day.

"I needed the caffeine," the customer said, pushing the cup at Mia. "And now I'd like the macchiato I ordered."

I pretended I wasn't eavesdropping as I flicked my eyes to Mia to find her clenching her jaw so hard, I could almost hear it.

"I'm not giving you a free drink," Mia said.

"Then I'd like to talk to your manager," the customer said,

and I couldn't see her face, but I could hear the smugness in her voice.

Mia closed her eyes and took a breath. "Tenley, you do this at least once a week."

"I know, and you get annoyed every time and then give me my drink, so why don't you just go ahead and do that," the customer said.

Oh. They knew each other.

Mia took the cup from the counter and threw it in the trash.

"Don't forget the extra caramel," the customer said in a sweet voice. "Thank you."

She went over to wait and then it was my turn. Mia made the other drink and then came over to me, her face red and splotchy.

"Sounds like you're having a rough one," I said.

"It's fine. That's just Tenley. We went to high school together and let's just say she hasn't changed. What can I get you?" I ordered three drinks and pulled some cash out of my wallet to shove in the tip jar.

I saw the infamous Tenley get her drink and then go back to her table, where she had a laptop open and a bag on the other chair.

"Thanks, Mia," I told her when I picked up my order.

"Thanks for not being an asshole," she said in a low voice.

～

"WHEN IS MIA MOVING IN?" I asked Sydney when I got back from my trip.

"Next week, actually. Lark somehow convinced me to help, and I don't really know how she did it except that she takes her boobs out and I will agree to just about anything," Sydney said and I snorted. The shop was empty for the moment, so we didn't have to worry about offending any customers.

"I know what that's like," I said. Ryan had absolutely fantastic boobs.

"Things are going good for you two?" Sydney asked.

"They're going," I said. "We're just dating and taking every day as it comes."

"So you haven't talked about the future," Sydney said, and I really wanted to get up and leave this conversation.

I didn't answer.

"Sorry, I'm being nosy. It's just that I have Layne breathing down my neck and dying to know how it's going. Ryan won't tell her anything and it'd driving her up a wall," Sydney said with a laugh. "Layne just hates it when people won't let her meddle."

"Tell her that she doesn't need to meddle. Ryan and I are both adults and we're figuring it out on our own. If I need help, I'll let her know," I said.

Sydney laughed again. "Yeah, that's not going to fly with Layne, but I'll try."

"Thank you," I said as a group of customers walked in.

∽

YOUR MAMA INVITED me over for dinner tonight Ryan sent me on Tuesday afternoon.

How in the hell did she get your number? I responded.

I sent her a message about maybe wanting to rent a house she replied.

They didn't say anything about it to me. I can tell them no for you I sent as I sat on my stool in the back of the pottery shop.

I already told her I'd come she responded.

Oh, okay. That's fine then. You can come over and have dinner and then we'll go to your place I sent.

Or we could just stay the night at your place she replied.

You sure you want to do that? I sent.

I think I can handle your parents. And your door locks, right? She responded.

It does I sent.

"Ryan is coming over tonight," I said to Sydney. "She's staying over and I'm trying not to freak out, but I think I'm freaking out a little bit."

"It'll be fine," Sydney said. "Your parents aren't that bad."

I let out a breath. "I really hope you're right."

Chapter Fourteen

"Please be normal," I begged my parents before Ryan arrived. "Just...don't be weird. Please."

Mama laughed. "Oh, you're being serious. We're not weird. Are we weird?"

Mom kissed her cheek. "We have our moments. Don't worry, we'll have dinner together and then get out of your hair. You can have the living room all to yourselves."

I wasn't going to tell her that we wouldn't need the living room since we would probably go right upstairs so we could do naked things.

"Okay," I said and then there was a knock at the door.

Ryan came in with more flowers, and she'd also brought cupcakes for everyone.

"They're chocolate cherry," she said.

"Perfect," I said, getting on my tiptoes to give her a kiss. "Come on in."

She set her bag down by the door and slipped her shoes off.

"Ryan, lovely to see you," Mama said, coming over to give her a hug and take the flowers.

"Thank you for inviting me," Ryan said.

Surprised By Her

"We're happy to have you," Mom said, taking some plates to the table in the dining room.

"Ohhh, they're getting out the fancy plates," I said to Ryan.

"What do you mean?" Mom said.

"Those are the plates we use for all the major holidays and birthdays," I said. "They're the fancy plates."

"They're not the fancy plates," Mama said.

"They're the fancy plates," I stage-whispered to Ryan.

"Can I help you at all, Lydia?" Ryan asked.

"You're the guest. Sit down and make yourself comfortable," Mama said. Ryan and I sat at the breakfast table and Mom brought Ryan a beer.

"Oh, thank you," she said.

"Bringing out the fancy beer," I said as she gave me one.

"This isn't the fancy beer," Mom said, shooting me a look.

"Beer is great," Ryan said, taking a sip and nodding. "It's good."

I tried it and it tasted better than the beer we normally had in the fridge.

"Fancy beer tastes better," I said.

"It's not fancy!" Mom said.

RYAN WAS a little quiet at the start of dinner, but then she warmed up and I saw the Ryan I adored when we were alone.

"How did you get into teaching?" she asked Mom.

"I always planned on being a teacher and a coach," Mom said. "There was never any other plan. Unlike some people who changed their mind a hundred times."

"Hey," Mama said. "It's not a crime to change careers a few times."

"A few dozen times," Mom said, and Mama scowled.

"I'm happy doing real estate now," Mama said. "I love

finding people their dream home where they'll make so many memories."

"I don't have a career," Ryan said, surprising me. "I mean, I don't have one anymore."

Mom and Mama shared a look.

"Before I got into selling real estate, I was working for a non-profit. I loved my job and I told myself the low pay didn't matter. I was helping people. I also ignored a lot of things that sent up red flags."

Mom raised her hand. "I saw the red flags, I'll have everyone know."

"Anyway," Mama said, taking Mom's hand and putting it down on the table, entwining their fingers together, "I stayed for far too long. It took me having a crying breakdown in the middle of a meeting, and a good long talk with my wife after, that led me to quit."

"Thank you," Mom said.

"Yes, thank you," Mama said, shooting an adoring look at Mom.

"My advice," Mama said, "is to sit down and imagine what you want your life to look like in five years, in ten years. Don't judge what comes up, just let it unfurl and see what it looks like. You might surprise yourself."

"Mama, you sound like a motivational speaker," I said, and she narrowed her eyes at me.

"Just because I heard it on a podcast, doesn't mean it wasn't good advice," she said.

"I'll try that, thank you," Ryan said.

RYAN REFUSED to not help with the dishes, and Mama wouldn't stop talking her ear off, but eventually Mom dragged her off.

"Have a good night," Mom said. "Forget we're even here."

"I plan to," I called as they walked up the stairs.

"Finally," I said, sitting next to Ryan on the couch in the living room. "Alone at last."

Ryan put her arm around me, and I leaned into her side.

"Your parents are so kind," she said.

"I know. They are. It's a lot to live up to," I said.

"I'm going to try that visualization thing," she said.

"It sounds corny, but sometimes that corny stuff works," I said. "I should probably do it at some point. I'm fine now at the pottery studio, but at some point, I'm going to need to find something that pays better."

"You will," Ryan said, her fingers stroking my arm up and down in soothing patterns.

"So will you. You're going to figure it out, Ryan," I said.

She put her finger under my chin and turned my head up so she could kiss me.

"We both will."

"WE HAVE TO BE QUIET," I said when we were in my bedroom later. "I'm serious, I cannot let my parents know that I'm having sex." It made me feel like I was going to die from embarrassment.

"Cupcake, I think your parents know that we're having sex," Ryan said, pulling her shirt over her head. "Are you going to let that stop you?"

She removed her bra and stood there, waiting for my answer. I sat on my bed and admired her glorious body.

"Hell no," I said. "Get over here."

Ryan grinned and leaned down to kiss me. "Good girl."

Very soon I wasn't thinking about my parents hearing us.

Ryan stripped my clothes from me, touching me all over as if she couldn't get enough of my skin.

"Your body is fucking perfect," she said. It wasn't nearly as perfect as hers, but I didn't say that. Instead I reached over to my nightstand and pulled out one of my favorite vibrators.

"We've tried yours, you wanna try mine?" I asked.

Ryan's eyes lit up.

"Absolutely. Hand it over." I relinquished control of the vibrator to Ryan, who took it in her hand and tested the settings. There were little metal beads in the shaft that spun and felt amazing when it was inside me.

"This is going to be fun," she said, dragging the vibrator down my body.

"Fuck, that feels good," I said, arching into the touch of the vibrator.

"It's going to feel even better very soon," Ryan said. "I'm going to make you feel so good, Everly."

Ryan kissed me as she moved the vibrator lower and lower.

"Ryan, please," I gasped as she teased my center with the vibrator. Her answer was flipping the vibrator to the next highest setting.

"SEE? It's not as good as your shower," I said as we bumped into each other for the third time. My shower wasn't bad, it just wasn't as roomy as hers. It didn't have a bench either, which was something I'd come to sincerely appreciate.

Ryan pressed me up against the wall. "Oh, I think it's all right."

I let out a whimper as her mouth descended on mine and her soapy hand stroked the sensitive area between my legs.

"I can't come again," I said into her mouth.

"You will, though," she said. "You'll come for me."

We both knew I would, but two could play at that game. I reached for her as well, finding her slick and ready. "Only if you come too."

"It's a deal," she gasped out as I thrust my fingers inside her.

∼

"IT'S WEIRD HAVING YOU HERE," I said as we lay in bed later. I knew I needed to sleep, but I was too busy staring at Ryan, holding her. Wondering how much time we had left together. She'd said she was staying the summer, but what did that mean? Did "summer" end in August? September? I both did and didn't want to know.

"Weird, good?" she asked. "Or weird, bad?"

"Definitely weird, good," I said, running my finger down the bridge of her nose.

"You know, your hair is fading again," she said.

"Wow, that's insulting," I said with a laugh.

"No, I mean, I can make you an appointment to get it done again," she said.

"You don't have to do that," I said, and at the same time I absolutely wanted her to do that. Making my hair appointments was a nightmare. My social anxiety extended to making phone calls, even for something as casual as a hair appointment.

"Let me," she said. "Just tell me when you want to go and I'll set it up and drive you."

I knew I should argue, but I didn't. I kissed her and said, "Okay."

∼

"GOOD MORNING, GIRLS," Mama sang when Ryan and I came down the next morning. I had to admit, waking up next to Ryan in my bed was amazing. Sure, her place was nice, but seeing her getting ready in my room, brushing her teeth in my bathroom, was a whole other feeling and I liked it. I liked having her in my space.

"Good morning," I said, stifling a yawn. "Are you going for a run?" I asked Ryan.

"No, I can wait," she said, but her body was twitchy. She loved her morning run before breakfast.

"Oh, if you want to go on a run, I'd be happy to go with you," Mom said. "You might have to slow the pace a bit and take pity on my poor knees, but I'm game."

Ryan hesitated for a second and then she smiled. "Sounds good."

She went back upstairs and changed into her running outfit and joined Mom, who wore her standard uniform of shorts and a T-shirt. I'd filled Ryan's water bottle that she'd brought with her and handed it to her.

"Have a good run," I said, tilting my face up for a kiss. "We'll have breakfast ready when you get back."

"Looking forward to it," she said, cradling my face and then kissing me softly.

Mom and Mama kissed and then the runners set off and I joined Mama at the stove.

"You two look very happy together," Mama said, almost vibrating with excitement.

"We're just having fun," I said. "It's not serious."

Mama set her spatula down and turned off the stove.

"Everly Candace, we both know that's a lie," she said, crossing her arms. "That girl looks at you like you're the sun. And you look at her the same way."

"It's just a summer thing. We haven't made any promises to each other. She's leaving. She's not going to stay here. She doesn't belong here." She belonged at the country club and in boardrooms and red carpets and helicopters. She didn't belong with me. We didn't belong with each other. Our worlds were too different.

"Sweetie, what you're saying doesn't line up with what I'm seeing. She adores you. What casual relationship would come and have dinner with her hookup's parents? She is literally on a run with your mom right now. That doesn't say casual to me. Not at all," she said.

I opened my mouth to argue, but she shook her head for me to stop.

"Just think about it. Let yourself imagine what would happen if it wasn't a fling. Don't dismiss the possibility of more just because you've put up imaginary roadblocks. You deserve someone who adores you, Everly. You deserve the best. While I think that no one is good enough for you, Ryan comes pretty darn close," she said. "Just think about it. Can you do that for me?"

"Yes," I said. I didn't tell her that I'd already thought about it. I'd woken in the middle of the night and had gotten up to use the bathroom. When I came back, Ryan was asleep, and I crawled in next to her. She'd made a noise and pulled me close to her, sighing in contentment.

I'd lain awake for a while, thinking about my life and how it would look if Ryan stayed. If we did this thing for real.

Mama would find us a place to rent and I'd continue to work at the pottery shop. Ryan would go back to school or find a job online or even take up something in Arrowbridge. She'd figure out what kind of career would set her soul on fire and she'd run every morning and come back and I'd have her breakfast ready. We'd go to the beach and on trips and maybe we'd get a dog. There would be birthdays and holidays and laughter and cupcakes. Maybe one day she would reconcile with her parents, maybe not. At least we'd have Mark and his wife and the twins as family. And Layne and Honor and Lark and Sydney and Joy and Ezra. My parents would help us plan our wedding and we'd all disagree about silly details. Someday there might be children, when we were ready. We'd go to parties and she would know exactly when I was ready to leave because she was so in tune with me because we'd been together so long. We'd be completely in sync.

It was a struggle to go back to sleep after that.

～

RYAN AND MOM were laughing as they came back from their run. Mom was definitely breathing heavier, but Ryan seemed happy anyway.

"I'm going to clean off really quick," she said.

"Did you have a good run?" I asked.

"I did," she said, giving me a sweaty kiss. "I'm starving, I'll be quick."

She ran up the stairs and I turned around to look at Mom.

"Well?" I asked.

"Well what?" she said, taking a glass of water from Mama and sitting down at the table.

"What did you talk about?" I asked.

"That's between me and Ryan," Mom said. "You can ask her."

"Rude," I said, pretending to glare at her.

Mom just laughed as Mama made up a plate for her.

～

RYAN CAME DOWN with wet hair and pink cheeks from the shower and loaded up her plate.

"You happy you got your run?" I asked.

"Yes," she said. She seemed lighter and more relaxed as she sat down next to me.

It was wonderful how ordinary it felt to have Ryan at our breakfast table. She wasn't out of place. She fit right into the fourth chair. Well, mostly.

"What are you doing for the rest of the day?" I asked her.

"I was somehow roped into taking the twins and their friends to the waterpark. Don't ask me how it happened, I'm not exactly sure. But I'm going. I haven't spent nearly enough time with them, so I think my guilt played a part in me agreeing to it," Ryan said.

"Oh my god, that sounds so…fun?" I said.

"You sound so enthusiastic," Ryan said, stealing a piece of bacon from my plate.

"No offense, but it sounds like my nightmare," I said. "Sorry."

"Do you want any tips? I've taken many, many field trips," Mom said.

"I might," Ryan said. "I'm not sure if I'm going to survive."

Mom sat forward. "Firstly, you're going to need to set the expectations from the beginning. Shenanigans will not be tolerated."

"I feel like I should be taking notes," Ryan said.

"Feel free," Mom said as Mama looked on adoringly.

"I love it when she goes all stern teacher," Mama said, wiggling her eyebrows.

"Ew, didn't need to know that," I said, but they all ignored me.

∽

"HAVE A GOOD DAY," Ryan said when she dropped me off.

"You are going to have to send me updates from the water

park," I said. "And if you start to lose your mind, just message me and I will make you feel better."

"You're the best," Ryan said, using my shirt to pull me in for a kiss. "I'll pick you up later."

"Bye, Ryan," I said, giving her one more kiss before hopping out of the car and blowing her a kiss.

Sydney was smirking at me from the front of the pottery shop when I unlocked the door.

"I saw that kiss," she said. "Looks serious to me."

"You sound like my parents," I said.

"Your parents sound like they agree with me, which means they're right," she said.

I wanted to argue with her. To tell her all the reasons that it couldn't and wouldn't work with Ryan, but there was that nagging in the back of my head. Mama's voice, telling me that I should imagine things working out.

I have quite a few regrets in my life, but this is the biggest Ryan sent me with a picture of her sitting in the front seat of an SUV crammed with tween girls.

You're not driving right now, are you? I responded.

No, we're officially at the water park and I'm trying to remind myself that this day will end eventually and I'll get to see your beautiful face again. It's been a rough day so far she sent.

I didn't look particularly cute, but I sent her a smiling selfie anyway.

I feel better already she replied.

Happy to help I sent.

RYAN'S DAY sounded like a nightmare, but it was pretty entertaining for me.

"I feel like Layne is the only one who could do that and

have a good time. She's magic with kids," Sydney said when I filled her in.

"Ryan seems to be holding her own. She adores the twins, and they look up to her, so I think that helps," I said.

"Ryan seems pretty great," Sydney said, readjusting the front window display.

"She is. She's the best," I said.

"Doesn't hurt that she's completely loaded," Sydney said.

"I don't care about that. The money doesn't matter to me. It's her mind and her smile and just…her everything," I said and found Sydney looking at me with a smug face.

"Interesting," she said.

"What?" I asked, feeling defensive.

"Oh, nothing," she said. "Can you hand me that lobster platter?"

Since I didn't want to talk about my feelings for Ryan with Sydney, I handed her the lobster platter and kept my mouth shut.

"YOU SURVIVED," I said when I hopped into Ryan's car.

"Barely, cupcake, barely," Ryan said. "Everyone got home in one piece and there were only three fights that I had to tag-team mediate with Layne's help."

"Hey, no blood or dismemberment? That's a huge win. I feel like we should celebrate," I said. "Did you want to go to your place for dinner, or come to mine?"

"How about we have dinner with your parents and then stay the night at my place? And then tomorrow we can switch," she said.

I gave her another kiss, nuzzling her face with mine. "I really like that idea."

So did my parents, who quickly stopped giving us privacy

and folded Ryan right into our family TV watching. I told her that we could go upstairs and watch shows in bed, but she said she didn't mind at all. Ryan and Mom had formed a friendship and every time we stayed at my place, Ryan and Mom got up in the morning and went for a run. Mama and I made breakfast, and we all ate together before going off to work. On nights when it was just me and Ryan, we most often cooked on the grill and ate outside if the weather was nice. If it rained, we would lay on the couch together and watch TV or she would read to me. We'd have sex and I got to try even more of the items in Ryan's toy box and found quite a few new things that I'd never thought of trying. She even placed an order for a few things to replace the ones that she had in storage.

The days went by with more fun dates and fancy dinners and champagne and book club and even more parties and dinners and days spent at the beach.

Our time together felt like a bubble that could burst anytime, and I didn't want to pop it by asking how long things were going to last, so I didn't. I kept my mouth shut, and it wasn't easy.

Chapter Fifteen

ONE SATURDAY in mid-August we had decided since it was raining all weekend that we would spend it reading together so we went to Mainely Books to grab a stack of books. I used to do this same thing alone, but it was way better doing it with Ryan. Sometimes she'd bake while I read, so when I took a break there were delicious treats waiting for me. And sometimes, Ryan would let me eat them off her abs.

"What do you think?" I said, handing her one of the books I picked out. It was the third in a contemporary romance series that was actually set in Maine. I was a complete sucker for a college student/teacher romance too.

Ryan read the back and nodded, putting it in her basket before pulling another book off the shelf.

"Oh, this sounds good too." I scanned the blurb on the back.

"Yes, give me an age gap with a doctor all day every day," I said. "Plus, the author was actually a surgeon before she started writing romance and she even formed her own publishing company. Totally badass."

"Agreed," Ryan said. "Definitely need that."

"How are your arms?" I asked her. The basket was pretty full.

"My arms can take it," she said, flexing for me.

"Okay, we need to get you home right now," I said, shoving her toward the register. There was a line, but I didn't mind.

There was a new face when we got to the front of the line. "Hey, Mia, are you working here now?"

"Just a few hours on Saturday," she said as Ryan set the basket on the counter. "Renting a new apartment and paying for it on your own can get expensive, apparently."

"I swear, I still have this panic on the first day of the month and it takes me a while to remember that I don't have to currently pay rent," I said.

"Tell me about it," Mia said with a laugh. She finished scanning our books and Ryan paid as I shoved the books first in my bag and then Ryan's.

Ryan went outside first and held the umbrella up so I could step under it.

"You're so thoughtful," I said, taking the hand that wasn't holding the umbrella.

"You're welcome," she said. "It's easy to be thoughtful with you."

Ryan even opened my door for me and made sure no rain got on me as I got in.

"You seriously don't have to baby me that much. I'm not going to melt if I get rained on," I said, checking the books and making sure that none of them got wet.

"I don't baby you, I just…" she trailed off and then turned on the car.

"You just what?" I said, pulling out one of the books.

"Nothing," she said, backing out of the parking space.

∽

Surprised By Her

"HAVE YOU TALKED TO HER YET?" Mama asked the following Monday morning as we made breakfast. Mom and Ryan were on their run, as usual.

"Mama, you've got to let it go," I said. This was probably the tenth time she'd pushed me to talk to Ryan about our future together. "Things are good and I want them to stay that way."

"Sweetie, I know you're happy, but I can tell when you're thinking about it. A mother knows. It's so much better to know than to sit in uncertainty, isn't it?" She pulled me into a hug.

"I just don't want you to have regrets. Your mom and I adore Ryan and we adore her for you. We'd be thrilled to add her to the family."

"Whoa," I said, pulling back. "You need to pump the brakes, Mama. Ryan isn't joining our family. We've only been dating for a few months, and like I have told you, she's not staying here," I said, yet again. I felt like I should record myself saying this so I could just replay it the next time she brought it up.

Ryan and Mom arrived home before Mama could launch into her advice again, for which I was grateful.

"Oh, Lydia, I have some news for you. I managed to find a case of those Fall Frolic candles in a random warehouse and they should be arriving next week," Ryan said, taking the cup of coffee that I handed her and giving me a kiss.

"Really?" Mama said, clasping her hands together.

"Yes, really," Ryan said, and Mama hurled herself at Ryan, who gave me the coffee back at the last minute so she didn't dump it all over the floor.

"Oh, thank you thank you!" Mama said, wiping tears. "I just love that scent so much."

"She really does," Mom said. "Thank you, Ryan. That means a lot."

"You're welcome. It was my pleasure," she said, sitting down to her breakfast.

"You know she loves you more now than she loves me," I told Ryan. "Thanks a lot for that."

"I still love you," Mama said.

"Uh huh," I said, glaring at her.

Ryan laughed and grabbed her coffee again.

"WANT to go to the beach tomorrow?" Ryan asked me that Friday night as we lay in my bed together after a particularly steamy session involving Ryan wearing a bespoke harness and a custom dildo she'd designed. Safe to say, the results had been mind-blowing.

"I'd love to," I said, tracing patterns on her back as she lay on her stomach.

"Maybe I'll get you in the water this time?" she asked.

"I'll get my legs in the water, does that count?" I asked.

"Mmmm, we'll see," she said. "I think I can convince you." She gave me a devious smile.

"If convincing me involves me being thrown into the ocean, then absolutely not," I said.

"But you're so easy to throw," she said, and I leaned down and gently bit her shoulder.

"Not all of us can be glamazons," I said.

"And not all of us can be fun-sized," she countered.

"If you throw me in the ocean, I will never have sex with you again," I said, trying to sound stern.

"Oh, in that case," Ryan said, sitting up and pushing me onto my back. "I won't do it."

"Thank you," I said, and our mouths met.

ONE BONUS of dating someone as tall and strong as Ryan was that I rarely had to carry anything that weighed more than ten pounds. She could also reach anything on top shelves for me. I'd gotten used to grocery shopping with her and not having to climb the shelves or suck it up and ask a stranger to help poor, short me.

Ryan carried nearly all of our beach stuff down the sand as I picked a good spot.

"Here," I said, pointing. "This is it."

Ryan dropped everything and then helped me set up the chairs and the blanket and everything else.

"I'm going to take a swim. Come with me?" Ryan asked, holding her hand out to me. I'd already sat down and pulled out my latest book, the professor/student romance.

"I'm coming to stick my feet in to soak up the ocean essence and then ogle you as you swim. Deal?"

Ryan laughed. "That works for me."

The water wasn't any warmer than I expected it to be, so I was not submerging my entire body in it. Ryan stayed with me at the edge of the waves until I pushed her to get in and swim. She did, and I marveled at her as she did her ocean laps and I just...stood there, watching this astonishing creature who somehow wanted to spend time with me. This summer didn't start out this way, but here I was, and I realized that I didn't just want this summer with her. I wanted fall, with apple picking and carving pumpkins with my parents. I wanted winter, with snowball fights I would lose and hot cocoa and books by the fireplace. I wanted spring with planting dozens of wildflowers that I'd pick for her. And then summer again, with beach days and sunburns and burgers on the grill.

I wanted it all.

"You okay?" Ryan said as she waded out of the water and I held her towel up for her.

"I'm great," I said, my voice a little choked.

Ryan shook her head like a dog and I screamed and darted away. She didn't let me get far before she picked me up and spun me around kissing me mercilessly.

"Come on, let's go find some wishing rocks," she said, taking my hand and dragging me down the sand.

Ryan walked next to me as we searched for rocks, but I was too busy having a mental breakdown over the fact that I was completely and totally in love with her.

This was terrible. I loved her and she was going to leave me here. I couldn't tell her. I shouldn't tell her. She could never know. Ryan could move on with her life and she would never know.

"Look," she said, pressing a rock into my hand. "It has two rings. How about we each get a wish?"

I didn't want wishes. I wanted her. I looked up into her face and remembered that I'd already wished for her once. I guess I hadn't been specific enough because I'd wished to have her and I had, but I wasn't going to have her forever. Curse you, wish parameters.

Ryan put her hand over mine, so the rock was sandwiched between our palms.

"Make your wish," she said, steeping close to me.

"You first," I said, looking up into her eyes. They were full of such rich intensity that I felt like I was going to cry.

I loved her. I loved her so much.

"There's only one thing I want," she said.

"What's that?" I asked, trying not to clench my hand around the rock.

She inhaled. "You. I want you, Everly."

"Me?" I said, blinking once.

"Yes, you. I love you. I want to be with you, and not just for the summer. I want to be us. Forever."

The rock dug into my palm as she held my hand tightly.

"I love you," she said again.

This couldn't be real. Was this really happening?

"What is it?" she asked, and I could feel her trembling.

"I wished for you," I said. "I wished for you at the beginning and I didn't think I'd ever have you. Are you sure?"

Ryan stared at me as if I was joking. "Of course, I'm sure. I love you."

"But I live here, in Arrowbridge. You hate it here."

Ryan scoffed. "I don't hate it here. You're here. And I like the beach. The rest of the town is growing on me. Good pizza."

"But you've got so much money. You could live anywhere, do anything," I said, and she put a finger to my lips.

"There's nowhere else I want to be than with you, Everly," she said.

When I didn't try and protest again, she removed her finger.

"Kiss me," I said, and she did, her mouth demanding and soft and aggressive and sweet all at once.

"I love you, too," I said, a few tears running down my cheeks. "I love you and I want to be with you."

Ryan exhaled shakily. "That's a huge relief."

"Is it?" I asked.

"Yes," she said. "Kiss me again."

I threw myself into her arms, the wishing rock falling from our hands. We didn't need it anyway.

Epilogue

"Cupcake, this is ridiculous," Ryan said as she stood on the porch of our new rental with her backpack. She shivered in the cold January air.

"Just smile," I said, holding up my phone. "This is your first day of school and we need to document it."

Ryan glared at me, but then she flashed a smile and I got a good shot.

"This is not my first day of school. I have a Master's degree," she said.

"Yes, but now you're going back, and I am going to celebrate," I said. "Now come and kiss me."

She did, lifting me up in her arms the way I loved. Things had changed incredibly fast for us. At the beginning of last summer we had just met, and now in winter we were sharing a home and Ryan was headed off for her first day of school to get her teaching certificate on the way to becoming a gym teacher and coach, just like my mom. They'd formed a bond that made my heart sing. Mama adored Ryan too, even more so when her candles had arrived.

I sent the picture to the group chat and my phone started blowing up with messages for Ryan.

"You should see these," I said, reading them.

"I put my phone on silent," she said, but I reached into her pocket and pulled it out. She smiled softly as she read through the messages from all our friends.

"This is ridiculous," Ryan said, but she was beaming.

"They love you," I said.

Ryan looked up from her phone and slid it back into her coat pocket.

"I love you, and I'm so grateful that I met you," she said. "I couldn't have done any of this without you."

"I love you, Ryan," I said, gazing into her blue eyes. "I'm so glad I spilled coffee on you."

She burst out laughing. "I'm glad I kissed you in that bathroom."

"We're never telling anyone that was our first kiss, right?"

She leaned down and our mouths met softly. "Never."

"Go on, you don't want to be late," I told her, shivering. "And I need to get ready for work."

Ryan's eyes sparkled. "What if we both played hooky?"

"You're not skipping your first day of school. If you skip school, you're grounded." I tried to put on a stern face.

"Mmmm, I like that. We can be grounded together. Naked." She reached down and squeezed my ass.

"That's not how grounding works!"

"It works for me," she said, biting my earlobe softly.

"No, go to school," I said, my protest getting weaker. If she didn't go soon, I was absolutely going to cave.

Ryan sighed. "Okay, okay. I'll go. But I'll miss you, cupcake."

"I love you," I said. I never got tired of saying it. I never would.

"I love you so much, Everly," she said.

THANKS SO FOR READING! **Reviews are so appreciated!** They can be long or short, or even just a star rating.

READ THE NEXT BOOK, Allured By Her where Mia agrees to be a fake girlfriend for Tenley, the most popular girl from high school that she used to hate to make Tenley's ex boyfriend jealous. Too bad she's such a good kisser...

Turn the page to read a teaser!

About Allured By Her

I never looked forward to coming into work at the Common Grounds coffee shop and seeing Tenley Hill sitting at her usual table with her laptop. The most popular girl from high school always seemed to harass me and try to get a free latte and was more infuriatingly pretty than ever.

Then one day she comes in and she's a total wreck. I make the massive mistake of asking her what's wrong. Turns out her boyfriend dumped her and all wants to do is try and get him back. Tenley pours her heart out to me and, for the first time, I see her as a person and not just the woman who annoys me every day. That moment of weakness causes me to agree to do something I never would have done under normal circumstances: date her. Well, pretend to date her. In public, wherever her ex will see us.

At first I hate the role of being a fake girlfriend, but soon I find myself flirting with Tenley and dreaming of her kisses. She's nothing like how I expected and before I know it, I'm falling for my fake girlfriend and I have absolutely no idea what the hell I'm going to do about it.

∽

"I ordered an iced macchiato, and this was hot," a voice said behind me. I'd been washing dishes in the sink and I had to grip it for a second before plastering a smile on my face and turning around.

"Tenley. You ordered a hot one. I know. I was the one who took your order," I said, trying to keep my voice even. I had a lot of regulars at the Common Grounds coffee shop, but Tenley Hill was by far the most irritating. At least once or twice a week, she came up to the counter and pretended that she'd gotten the wrong order in an effort to try and scam a free coffee out of us. I'd asked my boss, Liam, to ban her from the shop, but he said it wasn't a big deal and she did spend a lot of time and money when she wasn't scamming. Tenley was here at least three or four days a week for full days with her laptop. She did a lot of typing, but I had never asked her what the hell she was doing all those hours. I didn't want to know.

"Oh come on," Tenley said, leaning on the counter and letting her honey-blonde hair fall over her shoulder. "I *really* need it."

If I didn't know better, I would have said she was trying to flirt with me, but Tenley Hill would never flirt with someone like me. Girls like me didn't get flirted with by cheerleading captain prom queens.

She rolled her eyes. "Okay, fine, give me an iced macchiato. Extra caramel."

"Coming right up," I chirped in a fake voice. Tenley and I had gone to high school together and while she might not have given me the time of day, everyone knew who she was, and they still did around here. Tenley Hill could have anything she wanted, and I was not on that list. Besides, she had a hunky boyfriend that she talked to—often and loudly. No shocker that he'd been the captain of the basketball team. It was a match made in high school heaven. Gag.

I did my best to put Tenley out of my mind, which wasn't hard, since my job was so fast paced. Most days I barely got a minute to sit down, let alone think.

"She being her charming self?" my co-worker and friend Lark asked, bumping my shoulder with hers.

"Always," I said, rolling my eyes. "Can you grab me some more almond milk from the back?"

"Sure," she said, heading to the storage room. I made a few lattes and iced coffees and heated up scones before she made it back. "Sorry, Liam grabbed me for a second."

"It's okay," I said, taking the almond milk from her so I could froth it into a latte. Lark and I moved in tandem to make everyone in line happy, sliding by each other with the ease of practice. Sometimes our boss, Liam, said it looked like we were dancing. Having chemistry with your co-workers was so important when you were working in a confined space. Lark and I were a great fit.

There was a brief lull that let us take a breath and catch up on things we couldn't do when we were busy.

"No, Shane, I do not want to go house hunting with your mother," a sharp voice said, cutting through the soft jazz music that played all day.

Lark and I shared a look. Tenley was fighting with her perfect boyfriend for the second time this week.

"I should not be enjoying this, but I am," I said to Lark as Tenley continued to argue with Shane.

"Me too," she said. "I feel like I need popcorn." She pulled out her phone.

"You're not filming her, are you?" I asked.

"No, I'm sending a play-by-play to Sydney. She loves other people's drama," Lark said.

"I should probably tell you that management would frown upon you doing that, but I'm not going to," I said as Tenley continued to talk to Shane and gesture with her free hand. Things were not going well.

"Fine, Shane, that's just fine," she said, her voice in that deadly soft tone that just about anyone would recognize. She hung up and set her phone down on the table.

The other customers in the shop were all staring at her, but she didn't seem to be bothered. Tenley never seemed bothered by anything, not that I had seen.

She just went back to typing, but her jaw was clenched tight.

"Okay," Lark said with a sigh. "Drama over. For now."

"Yeah," I said, still looking at Tenley. Everyone else lost interest, but I saw her reach up and swipe away a tear before she started typing again.

"I wish I could have been there to see it," Sydney said as Lark made dinner that night. When I'd first moved in, they had insisted that I come over for dinner a few times a week and I'd caved due to the pressure from both of them. Lark was my best friend and Sydney was her girlfriend and it was two against one. Plus, Lark had become a really good cook and I got to sit on the couch and gossip with Sydney and pet their fluffy orange cat, Clementine.

"It wasn't the Fourth of July, but it was still pretty intense," I said. "If I didn't know her, I might have felt sorry for her."

"I barely know her, and I don't feel sorry for her," Sydney said. She'd been a few years ahead of us in school, so she hadn't had the misfortune of dealing with Tenley, but she'd heard enough from me and Lark that she'd formed a correct opinion.

"Oh, they'll make up and she'll be back to messaging him constantly and taking selfies to send him," I said. "People like that don't change."

Find out what happens next…

Reading List

Ash by Malinda Lo (Chapter Two)
  The Last to Leave by Erica Lee (Chapter Four)
  Legends and Lattes by Travis Baldree (Chapter Six)
  Champagne Problems by Addison Clarke (Chapter Fifteen)
  Only This Summer by Radclyffe (Chapter Fifteen)

About the Author

Chelsea M. Cameron is a New York Times/USA Today/Internationally Best Selling author from Maine who now lives and works in Boston. She's a red velvet cake enthusiast, obsessive tea drinker, former cheerleader, and world's worst video gamer. When not writing, she enjoys watching infomercials, eating brunch in bed, tweeting, and playing fetch with her cat, Sassenach. She has a degree in journalism from the University of Maine, Orono that she promptly abandoned to write about the people in her own head. More often than not, these people turn out to be just as weird as she is.

Connect with her on Twitter, Facebook, Instagram, Bookbub, Goodreads, and her Website.

If you liked this book, please take a few moments to **leave a review**. Authors really appreciate this and it helps new readers find books they might enjoy. Thank you!

Also by Chelsea M. Cameron

The Noctalis Chronicles

Fall and Rise Series

My Favorite Mistake Series

The Surrender Saga

Rules of Love Series

UnWritten

Behind Your Back Series

OTP Series

Brooks (The Benson Brothers)

The Violet Hill Series

Unveiled Attraction

Anyone but You

Didn't Stay in Vegas

Wicked Sweet

Christmas Inn Maine

Bring Her On

The Girl Next Door

Who We Could Be

Castleton Hearts

Mainely Books Club

Tempted By Her is a work of fiction. Names, characters, places and incidents are either the product of the author's imagination or are use fictitiously. Any resemblance to actual persons, living or dead, events, business establishments or locales is entirely coincidental.
No part of this book may be reproduced, scanned or distributed in any printed or electronic form without permission. All rights reserved.
Copyright © 2022 Chelsea M. Cameron
Editing by Laura Helseth
Cover by Chelsea M. Cameron

Printed in Great Britain
by Amazon